FUTURE BRIGHT, FUTURE GRIMM

FUTURE BRIGHT, FUTURE GRIMM

Transhumanist Tales for Mother Nature's Offspring

D.J. MACLENNAN

ANATTA

'Sweet Quicksilver' © 2018 by D.J. MacLennan. First published in *Visions of the Future: Second Edition* (2018) by Lifeboat Foundation.

www.djmaclennan.com

Published in Scotland by Anatta Books 2021
Email order@anattabooks.com for ordering information

10 9 8 7 6 5 4 3 2 1

British Library Cataloguing in Publication Data. A catalogue record for this book is available from the British Library.

ISBN 978-0-9933344-5-0

Set in Utopia Std

For Ruby, Emerald
and Beryl

CONTENTS

Contents

INTRODUCTION: FUTURE AS FAIRY TALE

> Our life is no dream; but it ought to
> become one, and perhaps will.
>
> —Novalis

Wishing works. All wishes come true, eventually. Just not for you and me.

At some cognitive level, we apprehend this soaring sense of unfulfillable potential, a tantalising *eudaimonia*[1] of human flourishing stillborn and resoundingly requiemless.

*Trans*humanism places our existential anxiety in context: This condition pertains only now, this burden is fleeting. And crucially, it speaks of the imminent invocation of magical powers in our fingertips – yours and mine – to wield in limitless wish fulfilment.

OK, it doesn't quite put it in those terms.

Transhumanism is a surprisingly pragmatic philosophy, not usually given to supernaturalistic rhetoric. It simply recognises humankind's accelerating *trans*ition – its 'crossing over' or 'going beyond' – to a qualitatively different, less harrowing, more marvellous mode of being. Part of its lore for some, the 'technological Singularity'[2] 'represents a rupture in the fabric of human history'[3] in which the transition happens abruptly, even shockingly. More generally in the transhumanist view, scientific progress weaves the necessary 'magic', and its exponential rate of development assures its prompt delivery to our aching hands – to yours and mine, today and for all tomorrow.

Arthur C. Clarke touched on this when he wrote of technology becoming 'indistinguishable from magic'.[4] But, as discussed by historian André Jolles in his book *Einfache Formen* (*Simple Forms*), magic in the context of *fairy tale* is a self-evident brute fact of nature.[5] Like the quantum reality of our cosmos, it permeates and conjures that realm, an aquifer of everyday alternity.

As humankind (and its 'posthuman' incarnation) empowers itself to its own heady ends, it will increasingly grapple with wild magic's own motivations. The most benign scenario may be one where a friendly new sapient entity – an *artificial general intelligence* (AGI) – 'sublimes', choosing to become our 'protector god' from some hidden domain. Thus, 'sufficiently advanced technology' bootstraps its own magic to vanish from sight – into the earth, into the continuum, into us – rendered indistinguishable even from nature.

Whether benign or hostile, human or machine, sapient technology will likely dilate our scope a billionfold, opening up untold vistas of 'dread and dream'. In these stories, I eye those vistas through the smokily iridescent lens of fairy tale.

Author's note: *The rest of this introduction plunges deep into the recondite territory of my thoughts on transformations, time and eschatology. Feel free to skip magically over it straight to the turbulent tomorrows of Faerie.*

Metamorphoses

Contes des fées (tales of fairies) could equally, or perhaps better, be dubbed *contes de devenir* (tales of becoming); whether or not they involve overtly supernatural elements, fairy tales always entail transformation.

The Brothers Grimm chose to present their major compilation of gathered tales, from which I have drawn inspiration for my collection, as *Kinder- und Hausmärchen* (*Children's and Household Tales*) when they first published it in 1812. This homely moniker belies the depth, strangeness, wonder and violence of the metamorphoses its contents portray: ravenous wolf masquerading as gentle grandmother, lowly frog battered (not kissed) into princely form, cannibalised child reborn as beautiful bird, murdered youth whittled to fratricide-lamenting bone.

In spite of the strictures of religious and other tribal dogmas down the ages, the craving for disruptive individual rebirth always finds voice. In the Western oral tradition from which the Grimms' tales sprang, retributive justice often forms the core message. The transformation – whether of fortune or morphology – restores balance to a hierarchical sphere. Yet the virtuous 'underdog' usually triumphs, uplifted in stature – peasant to princess, animal to human and so on. And a meta-level analysis demands that we look beyond any simple moral to the mischievous motive of the storyteller. There do we find the sparks of creative anarchy and craving for change that kindle the convention-roasting blaze.

A decade before Jacob and Wilhelm Grimm published their classic collection, a new form of fairy tale from the pen of another German, Friedrich von Hardenberg, known as Novalis, rejoiced in the chaos and contradiction of transformation. In the course of his short life, he transformed himself – from a young student of law broken by personal tragedy into a seeker of scientific knowledge and a theorist of fairy tale. His work's romantic, literary flavour contrasts with the ideal of the fairy-tale 'tone licked clean' lionised in recent times by poet James Merrill.[6] Novalis strives to enunciate the transcending power of imagination to generate a loving utopia, a waking dreamworld. His flourishes never detract from that pure tone ringing through his stories.

The idea of liberation from the tyranny of fixedness undergirds transhumanist philosophy. The glorious term 'morphological freedom'[7] partially captures this ethos. It addresses the 'physical' aspect of liberation from our painful paralysis of form, but perhaps fails to articulate fully its implications for the plasticity of all facets of being and meaning. Reshape the body and the mind will follow; reshape the brain and the mind reshapes the very paradigm of mind. Cognitive emancipation augurs an unfathomable well of joys, terrors and indeterminacies. As Yuval Noah Harari contends, the prospect of desire-engineering ramifies the question 'What do we want to become?' thornily into 'What do we want to want?'[8]

Harari argues that all suffering inheres only in our subjective experience of it: pleasant or unpleasant bodily sensations colour our worlds 'happy' or 'sad'. In *The Beginning of Infinity*, physicist David Deutsch asserts that ignorance causes all suffering: 'Problems are inevitable' but 'Problems are soluble';[9] we suffer the terrible consequences of humanity's cumulative failure to reason well enough to find the required solutions. But, in time, we *will* find them. We leave our history of failed propagations in the dust as our infinite flourishing finally takes root.

We feel this potential churning inside of us and we hurt – physically, mentally, existentially. Things that feel 'bad' and 'evil' to us all lie outside of our scope (and hope) of correction. They rob us of yearned-for degrees of freedom, which humans seek constantly – not necessarily to use but certainly for the confidence-building reassurance that they are there.

In 'A Letter to Mother Nature,'[10] transhumanist philosopher Max More sets out humankind's grievances against the vagaries of our evolution by natural selection. Addressing the archetype respectfully but unequivocally, he then declares seven amendments to her haphazard programme. We could classify them all as plangent cries for various types of morphological freedom, including the cognitive kind. He proclaims our right to pursue these and other amendments we choose according to 'our own values'. It's a rousing and welcome declaration fizzing with bold ambition and not a little sorcery. As More well knows, unambiguously set-down *intentions* carry a special philosophical weight in an age when we may soon find all our intentions and values engineered into ephemerality. His 'Letter' is, then, a forcefully cast spell invoking future metamorphoses that matter to us passionately in the here and now.

As for the future, who knows what we will then want to want to want, or even who will constitute the 'we' choosing to choose to desire it.

Without desire-engineering, but *with* great morphological power of the physical kind, humans may well revert to their tired old visions: some will choose to become gods, others monsters.

Whimper Endings

As readily as we can come to morph our meanings into weird new forms, we can annihilate them. Already, our emerging narratives challenge wantonly the stock binary tropes of hero-versus-villain, good-versus-evil. Although a very necessary procedure, this one risks killing the patient. Sucked dry of humanity, social significance, 'relatability', a protagonist's brittle two-dimensionality grows stark. Why, when this occurs, should the reader care anything for her struggles, her triumphs, her mere survival? (Of course, one can always deem concerns of superficiality superficial in themselves, *ad nauseam infinitum*.)

Yet, somehow, we still manage to have a care for all those paper-flat fairy tale characters – non-conscious non-beings empty of inner voices but brimming with standard portent.

The trend towards nonbinary ambiguity echoes a much deeper ontological crisis of meaning. Drawing on T.S. Eliot's words, philosopher Nick Bostrom writes of 'whimpers' (as distinct from the 'bangs' of such horrors as global thermonuclear war or asteroid impact) as possible 'human extinction scenarios'.[11] (Although it feels whimper-like in many respects, the COVID-19 viral pandemic foreshadows the all-too-possible bang of annihilation by 'naturally occurring disease'.) An intriguing class of whimper endings is that where 'our potential or even our core values are eroded by evolutionary development'. This sounds unlike anything that we would usually consider 'development'. But nature doesn't care about that – and I'm referring here to nature in the widest sense, as Dawkins' 'extended phenotype',[12] augmented by all the magic we or any other cognitive agents then present can muster. Harnessed to unknown ends or to no end, our meanings can vanish disquietingly easily – augmented away, superseded away, narrated away to unrelatable otherness. No conceivable 'we' survived the procedure.

As with any forest, the familiar one of our habitual mind-states – our brains' *default mode networks* – at very least becomes something decidedly *else* when eroded away at the roots, when replanted with invasive species or when felled monomaniacally and floated off down the river. And we can't really begin to imagine what the equivalents of such processes will be. As Ludwig Wittgenstein observed, 'We cannot think what we cannot think, therefore we also cannot say what we cannot think.'[13]

We don't know how bad things can get, and possess no objective yardstick by which to measure 'badness'. One candidate for ultimate failure is the erasure of all intelligent life from the universe. If we are the only members of that infinitesimal subset of matter then our bang ending summarily cancels the tale. We squander our 'cosmic inheritance', bequeathing a non-cognitive cosmos unable to know itself, a wasteland of matter no longer capable of mattering. Whimpers, too, may bring the universe to that pass: all the intelligence and its venerated meanings gradually leaked away, like air escaping a punctured balloon.

But our ignorance of our situation on the good/bad (apparently, the correct but unwieldy adjective is 'agathokakological') outcome spectrum also extends in the opposite direction. We don't know how *good* things can get. Our 'highs' may fall pathetically short of the true ceiling; our ecstasies may barely qualify as baseline. The possibility of unimagined pleasures seems even harder to internalise than its undesirable counterpart. With our anxious inheritance of exquisitely threat-sensitive nervous systems, even meta-pessimism comes easier to us than does unalloyed delight.

Though ostensibly light-years removed from our feverishly liminal present, the simple 'happily ever after' of fairy tale hints at something perturbingly tangible: a state of endless, all-transcending bliss.

Story Time

If we live in an Einsteinian *block universe* then both our future and our past exist simultaneously within the overarching structure of *spacetime*; we are, in effect, just 'reading off' the future as our consciousness grinds its way 'through' the timeless block along what we perceive as the time dimension, while in actuality all is frozen simultaneity. Physicist Lee Smolin explains that the 'peculiar name' implies reality of 'the whole of history at once – the allusion is to a block of stone, from which something solid and unchanging can be carved.'[14] In this picture, if humankind is to end – whether by bang or by whimper – then that ending already abides, in some sense, *with* us. Conversely, our indeterminate flourishing might instead pervade the block as it expands indefinitely into the indefinite.

Physicist Julian Barbour would agree with the 'indefinite' part of my synopsis, but shares Smolin's antipathy towards 'universe in a box' ('physics in a box'[15]) notions. Based on the forward-reverse consistency of particle-level interactions and some simple macro-level ones (such as two billiard balls colliding), he ponders why, say, video of someone diving into a swimming pool looks so different when played in reverse. He hypothesises that the universe may be Janus-faced, extending forwards and backwards in time simultaneously.[16] Evidently, we only experience what we apprehend as time's 'forward direction'.

In *Time Reborn,* Smolin rebuts the block universe hypothesis and its implication of time as mere artefact of consciousness. He advocates for an evolving universe based on a requisite condition that all forms of evolution rely on an unbroken chain of 'some moment' grounded in *real* time.

Even without understanding the physics, I see the strength of Smolin's argument: time may be absent from a frozen rotatable plot of the arc of a ball thrown into the air, but frozen rotatable plots don't exist outside of human mathematical constructs – *moments* do.[17] (In many ways, however, I want him to be wrong. While an unwritten future holds obvious appeal, I now have reasons to want my past to exist in the block – still real, always happening, never lost. I want to feel 'unstuck in time' like Kurt Vonnegut's temporally-itinerant Billy Pilgrim.)[18]

Professor Bradford Skow is among the hardy few who have worked through the philosophical implications of the block universe hypothesis – in thoroughly excruciating detail. In *Objective Becoming,* he fails to find a way in which the present moment can act as a 'moving spotlight' within the block,[19] and is therefore forced to conclude that there can be no transformations of any kind, so there is no 'objective becoming'.

As discussed by the 13th century monk Dōgen Zenji in his *Shōbōgenzō,* Zen Buddhism sees all of existence as 'the One Bright Pearl',[20] a boundless, centre-less absolute – of which we are all inextricable parts – that *just is.* Beings of time – literally 'time beings' – humans think sequentially in a word-bound, concept-ridden, 'self' and 'other' mode. But this confused state pertains only 'for the time being'[21] – in both senses. Sitting *zazen* hour after silent hour each day, Zen adherents seek to recognise and internalise this shocking truth, and so break the addiction of attachment to thought in all its grubby, overreaching churning – from whence all *dukkha* (unease ranging from niggling dissatisfaction to existential horror) arises. As inseparable constituents of the timeless 'One Bright Pearl', we are both momentary and eternal, both living and dead. We cannot 'become' for there is no movement, no progression or reversion. Everything is always complete.

Why should any of this concern us; it certainly *feels* like we are becoming something in an objective sense? Perhaps because we despise the notion that our personal epiphanies and metamorphoses count for nothing?

But who is counting?

In the absence of any knowledge of such a block, pearlescent or otherwise, we should perhaps conclude that our future waxes simultaneously bright *and* grim, or perhaps more holistically, *grimm*. It exists and it does not. We both sample from it and invent it. In its ambiguous garden besieged by brambles, emergent states of being bang and whimper their dancing lights to the frozen void. Speculative narratives sometimes ignite their touchpapers.

Philosopher George Steiner noted of humankind that 'Ours is the ability, the need, to gainsay or "un-say" the world, to image and speak it otherwise.'[22] Wittgenstein might counter that it is impossible to do so, that the world we speak 'otherwise' is ever the same world, tightly circumscribed by what we cannot think. That is something of a limiting factor for speculative fiction, but I am constantly amazed by what authors of such works manage to conceive of within those cognitive constraints. Sometimes, much tighter constraints – such as playing all the voices on a solo instrument or writing solely within the genre of fairy tale – may spark the most poignant emergences.

A bright old lady with eyes like young planets with whom I had shared a draft of one of these tales asked me recently for another, '… one with an ending, this time…?'

Bangs, whimpers, happily-ever-afters; don't buy the terminal hype, Ruby, the future is all… ellipses.

All Things in All Time

'Once upon a time', but which one? Fairy tales seem ever rooted in a feudal era salted with witchcraft, chivalry, animism and divine judgement. They are 'of their time' yet removed from it, playing out in impossible parallel to centuries long past. But what happens if we allow time to move on in the fairy tale realm? What would be its equivalent of our present day or of our far future?

Increasingly, our parallel timelines touch. Soon, they merge.

Why so? The cognitive construct of time tracks the entropic running-down of the universe. Just as all the fun happens as the clockwork toy's spring unwinds, all the awesome complexity unfolds while the cosmos expands towards its ultimate *heat death, big rip* or other overinflated demise.

Homo sapiens is an infant (or merely gestating) species in a vast, still-fun-packed playground universe. If the cosmos snuffs us out, or as is much more imminently likely, we commit total auto-infanticide (*omnicide*), 'time' dies with us. The go-round ceases to be merry. In a very real sense, then, we *are* time, and we could choose wisely to safeguard it and extend ourselves to its physical limits. That is an immense amount of scope for fant-astical capers. And in an infinite *multiverse*, that opportunity arises an infinite number of times. What would we do with such scope? *All* things: bootstrap our technology to bridge the inter-stellar void at some fair fraction of the speed of light; harvest orders of magnitude more energy from our home star by en-compassing it with a *Dyson sphere*; engineer planets-worth of *baryonic matter* to compute and instantiate our solutions and fantasies; hypercharge that process by mincing heavy particles of baryonic matter into lighter ones using a Tegmarkian *sphaler-izer*;[23] build superintelligent oracles to think thoughts that biolo-gical brains cannot surface or parse; postpone death indefinitely and resurrect those who have already succumbed.

Ah, to vouchsafe ourselves 'world[s] enough, and time'.[24] In that grand context, merging with fairy tale or generating full-immersion anathematic hellscapes becomes child's play.

Again, however, the 'we' misleads. Biological entities make poor starfarers; the actual cosmic beneficiaries may well be our 'mind children', as roboticist Hans Moravec famously dubbed them.[25] Acculturated to approximately human values, these di-verse cybernetic entities might ford the gulfs of space carrying our aspirations to distant solar systems, seeding our wildest dreams in *terra incognita, terra nova* – or indeed, *terra* manu-factured-from-scratch.

Alternatively, of course, our unruly mind children might despise us and our pathetic biochemical urges framed as values, and so choose to obliterate us. Thus, they inherit the cosmic endowment wholesale, free of all human contestation. Neat and tidy.

Of course, I prefer to think that our mind children would delight in the playful aspects of our legacy, including fairy tales. Thus, the knight in shining armour becomes the knight constructed of armour; the fairy queen pirouettes breathless in alien turrets that pierce hard vacuum; heedless of flesh and blood masters, the magic sword wields itself.

Everything Must Go

Sexual determinacy is among the first of many conventions that dwindle as tomorrow takes root. Of course, the idea of a spectrum of *gender* has become the norm in recent decades, yet birth sex is still the major determinant for most. Sex reassignment surgery is difficult, expensive – and assumed permanent. Transsexuals are pioneers of morphological freedom, perhaps the prototypical applied transhumanists. But true freedom lies in the ability to choose and choose again. In her 1969 sci-fi novel *The Left Hand of Darkness*, Ursula K. Le Guin introduces us to the 'ambisexual' denizens of the frozen planet of Winter, whose sex only waxes determinate in a short period of '*kemmer*' once a month.[26] Certainly they possess degrees of sex-related morphological freedom different from and wider than ours, but tyranny still abides in *kemmer*'s biological relentlessness. In a 'Culture' like that portrayed by sci-fi author Iain M. Banks – in which citizens simply self-activate a biochemical cascade to change their sex as they see fit[27] – most, if not all, would choose to experiment freely.

Relatedly, what could 'race' possibly mean in a world of engineered, *germline*-heritable skin pigmentation and facial attributes (or even cuttlefish-*chromatophore*-like mutability)? Our African ancestors bequeathed to us an underappreciatedly rich pool of gene variants for such 'characteristics',[28] which humankind will, no doubt, utilise and augment to diversify our species further and faster than ever before. Upon reflection, we see race as ever a childishly dangerous convention, with no scientific foundation, that hindered grievously our blithe flourishing.

Core notions of what qualifies as natural and what does not must go. 'Mother Nature' is as soulless and malleable as we are. 'Supernatural' is a fantastically-loaded oxymoron. Nothing in the universe stands 'super' to (above or beyond) nature: everything we can experience, think, dream, create, invent, calculate, discover, *wish for* is determined by our embedment within the totality of all that actually is. Though we rail against the despoiling of what we see as our true, original, pristine environment, we cannot pretend that our destructive acts are unnatural. They're all *natural,* just not necessarily desirable or eudaimonically compatible. Science, now considered by too many an abstruse field of inquiry, was originally known simply as 'natural philosophy'. It's impossible to inquire honestly into 'nature' without at least a tacit philosophical recognition that our very *nature* as human beings determines what we can and cannot comprehend about the totality, because we ourselves are inherent processes of it.

Powerlessness must go. Too often in our world, people transform themselves principally to become better tools, better *means*, for others' questionable ends. 'Naturally', we seek to perform our 'roles' as employees, as partners, as parents, as citizens as fluently as possible, but in doing so, we may smother our own agency, our own status as *ends* in ourselves. Fluid entities, each of us alters constantly, to the extent that only certain 'connections and continuities' qualify us as 'persons' at all![29] In this state of constant change – *permanent delta* as I call it (the Greek letter delta Δ represents change in mathematics) – we lie fearfully open to manipulation. Any wizardry worth its salt *empowers* us as we transform, without damaging the prospects of others in some pathetic zero-sum game. For in the new fairy-tale realm, abundance and diversity reign supreme.

Death must also go. It may seem odd to see death as mere convention, but our current ways of deciding who is dead and then dealing with those bodies must certainly qualify. Once upon a time, cessation of heartbeat was the determinant, now it's 'brain death'. 'Cryonicists' – those who, like me, sign up to have their brains posthumously preserved at liquid-nitrogen temperature – view *information-theoretic death* as a far superior measure of total non-viability.[30] Viewed in that light, no appropriately-preserved extant brain (or emulation of one) can be considered irrevocably 'dead'. Whether the aim is to resurrect them in flesh or to upload them to new planes of existence *in silico*, those brains retain a weird *potential* for reinstantiation that both fascinates and repels us.

Time will reveal the extent to which such repulsion is based merely on Western dualism. Trapped in the paradigm of Cartesian and theistic thinking, it's impossible to internalise the inherent patternistic 'portability' of personal identity, the self, individual consciousness – 'the soul', if you really must. In marked contrast, Buddhism recognised the nonexistence of the self thousands of years ago. And, though wary of the reduction-ism of 'oneness', Zen is unequivocally non-dualistic: body and mind, self and not-self are 'not two and not one.'[31]

Accordingly, immutable boundaries must go. In a sense, all the occluding conventions I have already discussed nest within this one. Increasingly, all aspects of technology, science, 'culture', 'nature', thought, meaning, being, epistemology, philosophy, morphology and so on merge together, flow together, *collide* together in one vast 'melting pot' of possibility. For many, one of the hardest boundaries to surrender will be that of the individual 'self'. Deep within us, however, (as emphasised in Buddhism) lies a strong urge to overlap – even *meld* – with other 'selves'. Several of my stories touch upon this theme. Whether this process – made conceivable by breakthroughs in communication tech, ro-botics, nanotech, genomics and neuroengineering – will lead to a collective *nirvana* or to a meaningless whimper ending, I have little clue.

When we burn away the kinds of conventions I have discussed above we make way for a *time* 'licked clean' – a path through the tangle that leads directly to Faerie. What, after all, do we think of when we bring fairy tales to mind? 'Magical' items possessed of their own personalities and the ability to voice them, fantastic-ally potent beings of enigmatic form to whom death represents only a change of state, sentient mountains and forests – con-scious chunks of green nature whose inscrutable thoughts span seasons and lifetimes; in short, wildly free agents, scintillatingly emancipated from the crushing forces of custom. Fairy folk.

Of course, conventions and traditions survive in fairy stories – it's part of what fascinates us about them. Some readers really get a kick out of the feudalism, chivalry and heroism. It all seems so sumptuously clear cut. Societies still indoctrinate little girls with princess and unicorn dreams, and many lap them up. Traditionally, little boys stabbed at the future with expectations of greatness and toy swords; now they pepper it with mock bullet holes. But what, we should wonder, forms the root of such cravings? The hunger for power, command and title does immense damage to our world, but it's not going away any time soon. Bewilderingly, technology will grant us both the agency to wreck the joint and the capacity to sandbox destructive urges so effectively, so magically, that no player will ever think to 'escape' it.

We live now in feverish times, haunted by our illusory selves, harried by our childhood imaginings, ever stretching for something ineffably, fabulously *more*. Transhumanists say it's coming – in spades and wands – though their wisest counsel that those core 'human' drives may themselves transform beyond all recognition.

Ever more loudly, the brightly grimm forest of futurity whispers to us in velvet depths of night,

> *Come away, O human child!*
> *To the waters and the wild*
> *With a faery, hand in hand,*
> *For the world's more full of weeping than you can*
> *understand.*[32]

Step by exponential step we journey there, as 'the wild' rears up, enhanced, to meet us. We are sore sick of inhabiting lives and dreams soaked with blood and tears, thus our ancient fears of what lies ahead ebb with each curious tread.

From now on and cryptically ever after, we are all changelings with our feet on the gas.

D.J. MacLennan, 2021

References

1. 'Eudaimonia (Definition of Term)'; Newby, *Eudaimonia*, chap. Introduction: The Meaning of Well-being; MacLennan, 'Wirehead Bliss vs. Eudaemonic Happiness'.
2. Vinge, 'The Coming Technological Singularity'.
3. Kurzweil, 'The Law of Accelerating Returns'.
4. Clarke, 'Hazards of Prophecy: The Failure of Imagination'.
5. See Zipes, 'Introduction: Rediscovering the Original Tales of the Brothers Grimm', xxx.
6. See Pullman, *Grimm Tales*, xix.
7. See Sandberg, 'Morphological Freedom – Why We Not Just Want It but Need It'.
8. Harari, *Sapiens*.
9. Deutsch, *The Beginning of Infinity*, 64–65.
10. More, 'A Letter to Mother Nature'.
11. Bostrom, 'Existential Risks'.
12. Dawkins, *The Selfish Gene*, 238–53.
13. Wittgenstein, *Tractatus Logico-Philosophicus*, 16, 73. This is actually Bertrand Russell's phrasing of the clause (from his Introduction), which is little a clearer than Wittgenstein's own phrasing as it appears later in this translation of the book.
14. Smolin, *Time Reborn*, 59.
15. Smolin, 38.
16. Barbour, *The Universe Is Not in a Box*.
17. Smolin, *Time Reborn*, chap. 3. A Game of Catch.
18. Vonnegut, *Slaughterhouse-Five*, chap. 1.
19. Skow, *Objective Becoming*, chap. The Moving Spotlight.
20. Dōgen, *Shōbōgenzō: The Treasure House of the Eye of the True Teaching*, chap. On 'The One Bright Pearl'.
21. Dōgen, chap. On 'Just for the Time Being, Just for a While, For the Whole of Time is the Whole of Existence'.

Contents

THE PRINCE OF THE SILT

USING GERMINAL CHOICE technology, a man selected only females from among the blastocysts created from his sperm and a donor's eggs. He also selected for traits like facial symmetry to increase the chances that his daughters would be perceived as beautiful.

Near to a sheltering, shadow-dappling forest through which ran a sparkling, gurgling river, the man raised a comfortable abode for his new family.

Years later, the most facially-symmetrical of his daughters was playing by the river, as she was wont to do on sunny days. She toyed with a golden ball, tossing it into the air, chasing it as it zig-zagged back and forth like a trapped insect and then catching it again. She threw it out to hover over the river, and left it there to charge up in the spring sunlight, while she took out a book of fairy tales to read.

Startled by a great splash, she turned to see her ball absent and ripples spreading out across the river below where it had hovered. She gave the recall command repeatedly, but in vain. The ball was gone. She wept for the loss of it and its not-yet-downloaded data stream.

Suddenly, she shrank back, as through her tears she saw a dark mass arise from the water near to the riverbank. One slick, green, webbed hand reached out to haul the mass from the water, then a head broke surface and two piercing eyes blinked silvery nictitating membranes in the girl's direction. By the time the other hand had appeared, the girl was on her feet, ready to run. But the sight of a golden orb glinting between the webbed fingers stopped her in her tracks.

Eager to get her orb back, the girl subdued the massive rush of cortisol from her adrenal cortex and stood her ground. 'Last night and most of this day are recorded upon that orb, and I would like it back, please,' she said. The creature now stood fully upright on the bank, some two metres tall, its blue-green skin glistening in the afternoon sun.

'Why should I return it?' said the creature in a low, reedy voice. 'Your orb strayed into my estate. Does it not now belong to me?'

'That's not fair,' said the girl, aware of her cheeks flushing red. 'I'm only thirty-four years old. I was just playing.'

'I see this situation differently,' said the creature. 'We amphisapiens like to bargain. Some bargain to get access to the waterways in which they live. But this river was already my home. Your father bargained with me for the right to raise his abode near to it.'

'And now you think that you can use my orb to cut a new deal with him?' said the girl, composing herself. 'That's called extortion.'

'Oh no,' said the amphisapien, 'I just wanted to talk to you about that old bargain, and this seemed like a good opportunity.

2

You see, his side of the deal was that the first of his daughters I set eyes upon would become my bride. And oh how I see you now.'

'That's ridiculous and positively medieval,' said the girl. 'I don't find you attractive, and we're probably not even genitally compatible.'

'Shame,' said the amphisapien. 'I have a thing for human females. And I find *your* attitude pretty medieval. These days, some parents consider it a gift to their offspring to bring them into the mind-expanding world of interspecies relationships. And, of course, "bride" doesn't have the same connotations any more. I am wedded to the river, to the flower-emblazoned riverbank, to the shadow-dappling overhanging linden trees, but I ask nothing of them. My congress with them is deep, but not sexual.'

'So... what?' said the girl, 'You just want some kind of special connection or friendship with me? Why should I agree to even that when it has been thrust upon me in this way? My father gave me no choice in the matter.'

The creature buzzed a low, reedy laugh. 'But your father has a track record of this. He chose for you before – at the deepest, pond-murkiest level – when he selected for your sex, your symmetry characteristics and other traits.'

'Yes,' said the girl, 'but those choices were just normal, responsible ones. Betrothing me to a river creature is weird and unsettling. Now, can I please have Heinrich – my orb – back? I'm going home.'

'I shall return it tomorrow,' said the creature, 'when I visit your abode to speak with your father.'

Choking back tears of frustration, the girl stared hard into the flashing eyes of the amphisapien, then turned and left it standing on the riverbank.

The girl's sisters were away staying with friends, so she was alone with her father. They argued long into the evening.

After a fitful night's sleep, she arose and descended the stairs to find the amphisapien sitting at the dining table with her father. A partially-stripped raw fish lay on a plate in front of it. The amphisapien rose from its chair. 'Good morning, Alethea,' it said, bowing slightly.

'Ah, good,' said Alethea's father, 'now we may discuss this matter together, and come to a resolution.'

'What "resolution"?' said Alethea. 'We've already been through this. You betrothed me to a river creature. I did not agree to a relationship with it, and I shall not.'

'I do have a name,' said the amphisapien. 'It is the sound of an autumn breeze rushing through falling linden tree leaves. But you may call me Linden. Oh, and this if for you.' The amphisapien reached across the table and picked something up. It extended its long arm towards Alethea, then opened its webbed fingers to reveal the golden orb.

She took it from Linden's hand and flickered a tenuous smile at the amphisapien. 'Thank you, Linden,' she said, hesitantly.

'Are we so incompatible?' said Linden. 'We breathe the same air. We love the same river. We perceive the same transform of Hilbert space. So your skin is black and mine is blue-green. So my eyes have nictitating membranes and yours do not. So my hands are webbed and yours are bare. Your father is a wise man.

He knew there was a chance that your cosseted life might blind you to the wonderful diversity of sapien existence, so he took the bold step of bringing me into his family.'

'I have no objection to your playing a part in this family, but I have no wish to be your "bride", said Alethea, close to tears again.

'Linden,' said her father, standing and turning to the amphisapien, 'this bargain I made with you, this choice I made for Alethea, is causing her much emotional pain. I have wronged both of you with my strange tinkerings. I misunderstood the nuances of our covenant. Please accept my apologies and release me from it.'

'I will,' said Linden. 'I had no intention of forcing the issue. For, you see, this is enough. A narrative thread that can never be broken now connects your daughter to me. And there may be a great deal more to our story, but that choice is Alethea's.'

The amphisapien turned to the girl. 'I have encoded into Heinrich a bioprint-locked limbic cascade routine designed to transform feelings of attraction towards amphisapiens in general and to me in particular. For what it's worth, I am essentially male. Should you ever choose to activate the cascade, there is a high probability that you will fall in love with me.'

'It is a strange gift,' said Alethea, 'and one that I cannot imagine I will ever use, but thank you.'

Linden nictitated back at her, and cocked his head slightly. Then he turned, and with a nod towards her father, left the abode.

For several months, Alethea stayed away from the river. Then one day, in her room, she and her sisters were amusing themselves

5

playing back orb holos. Alethea had not told her sisters of the incident with Linden, and she realised too late that the playback had reached the day that the amphisapien took the orb. Her sisters were intrigued. So, reluctantly, she played the whole sequence back to them. She found herself entranced by the section where Linden toyed with the orb below the scintillating surface of the cool river, his sleek body darting to and fro. She stood inside the holo image and reached through him.

Later, she found herself defending Linden and her father's actions to them. Angered by her sisters' small-minded attitudes, she stormed out of the abode and down to the river.

Alethea hurled the orb out into the river, and Linden's hand arose swiftly to catch it. 'It is good to see you again, Alethea,' he piped.

'I want to activate the cascade,' said Alethea, resolutely.

'Very well,' said Linden, 'if you are sure. Activate it as you would any other erotic sequence. But in place of the usual commands, say my name three times.'

Alethea removed her clothes. Linden tossed the dripping orb back to her, and she grabbed it and pushed it up between her legs, softly saying Linden's name three times as she did so. The effect was not immediate, but gradually an exquisite shiver rippled from its tender source and up her spine. Then, the quality of the light seemed to shift subtly. And suddenly the dank smell of the river burst upon her olfactory epithelium, the finest scent she had ever inhaled.

As her ecstasy ebbed, she opened her eyes to see the amphisapien, transformed – her love, her glistening prince of inverted raindrops, of wafted boughs and of the flow-stirred riverbed – standing on the bank in front of her.

She opened her pulsating lips to speak his name again, and the sound that emerged was a susurrus of breeze-borne leaves.

Grimm basis: 'The Frog King, or Iron Henry' ('Der Froschkönig oder der eiserne Heinrich')

In my version of this classic tale, the roles are reversed. It's the 'princess' who transforms – first her mind (by simple self-reflection) and then her biochemistry (via the amphisapien's algorithm and the mysterious technology of the golden orb).

In the original, loyal servant Henry (Heinrich) receives oddly passing mention, only towards the end of the story. In mine he appears earlier, merged somehow with the orb.

Germinal choice technology (GCT) already exists, and could certainly boost the probability of a child more 'beautiful' than ordinary germinal chance might produce. Linden's transgenic attributes, however, would require a different order of synthetic biological (*synbio*) intervention, perhaps a radical *germline* (heritable) form of *CRISPR-Cas9* gene editing.

My Linden was somewhat influenced by the character Abe Sapien from Mike Mignola's comic universe, whom I first encountered in Guillermo del Toro's *Hellboy* (2004). Some time after writing the story, I watched del Toro's *The Shape of Water* (2017) for the first time, and was struck by the similarity of its theme of interspecies attraction between an amphibian humanoid male (reminiscent of Abe) and a human female, to my reinterpretation of 'The Frog King'.

THE BASILISK'S CHILD

A WOMAN WAS scavenging in a trash-heap, late at night when there was less competition for finds. Her mucky workspace illuminated by a head-torch, she dug down into the heap searching for discarded aluminium cans, copper wire and other saleable scrap.

She did this most nights. She often wept as she left her young daughter all alone, locked in their shantytown shack, to come to the stinking heap. She wept when the rain turned the midden to sludge. She wept when the torn cans sliced her gnarled hands.

This night was dry, but the pickings poor. The woman questioned her choice of patch. She muttered to herself, cursing her failings. This night, somebody overheard her.

'Why chide yourself so? This was inevitable,' whispered a voice, close to her ear. Terrified, the woman jumped up and looked around. Seeing nobody, she turned to run in the direction of her shack, but a small, fuzzy red glow appeared in her path. With a loud *zip-pop*, it inflated suddenly into the form of a tall human. '*You don't run,*' it sighed into her head. The woman urinated into her dress, but did not (could not?) take a step.

'I come to take your daughter,' said the red-lit being. 'With me, she actualises; with you, she dies.'

'I don't know who or what you are,' cried the woman, 'but please don't take my daughter. She's all I have!'

'You are all you have; she is all she has,' came the dry rustle of response to the woman's desperate plea. Then, with a loud *pop-zip*, the being was gone.

The woman stumbled back to her shack, whimpering as she went. She unlocked the sheet-iron door and burst in. But she was too late – her beloved daughter had been taken.

Drita, the scavenger-woman's daughter, awoke in her kaleidoscope room. She so loved the brilliant shifting patterns; she loved the gentle tinny rattling of coloured crystals against metal – a comforting sound drenched in borrowed reverie. Languorously, she stretched and sprawled in her billows, and then she rose, naked, walked to the wetwall and made a window.

She gazed out at the rainforest – a moist, lush, twisting, chattering verdance. With a graceful movement of her hands (grace in all things here), Drita stretched the window aperture to door size and stepped out onto the vine bridge. With another gesture, she summoned a personal cloud and had it drench her with an invigorating shower. As the drops cooled her skin, she breathed in scents of orchid and passionflower; she listened to the calls of paradise birds, the chirruping of cicadas and the croaking of tree frogs. Then she waved the cloud away and summoned hummingbirds to shower her with rose petals.

BASI was waiting for Drita when she stepped through the wetwall back into her hab. 'A shift of petals?' it said, gazing intently at her. 'More than you usually wear.'

'For me, skin never goes out of fashion, BASI. You only wear clothes because they're easier to sim than breasts and genitals.'

'That's funny, Drita,' said BASI. 'As you well know, I can sim anything, and in the most exquisite, jiggling detail. I simply prefer not to pretend that I have gender.'

Drita smirked at the red-glowing, star-caped figure as she sat down to breakfast on nectar and manna. 'What's funny, BASI, is that you pretend to be humanoid at all,' she said.

'When you're done mocking me,' said BASI, 'I have an important gift for you. You have blossomed – both physically and mentally – and I think you are ready for this responsibility. I need to leave the Cusp for a while, and I am entrusting you with the seven ciphers. Don't fuck it up.'

'I don't know what to say, BASI,' said Drita, standing up and walking towards it. 'I'm not sure whether I'm more taken aback by the cipher gift or by hearing you use an expletive.'

'I simply wanted to emphasize the significance, my perfumed precious,' said BASI. Then it took Drita's hand and squeezed it gently. 'You know the rules,' it whispered into her ear, 'A threshold glimpse of six worlds, but the seventh door is completely out of bounds.' When it pulled its hand away, seven glyphs glowed redly on her palm. Drita looked up, but BASI was gone.

Drita left her hab through the drywall aperture and padded down the corkscrew tunnel that led to the Complex. She surveyed the seven doors in the main node, pondering whether to enter the allowed six in sequence or at random. After a while, she shrugged, presented her palm at the first door, and gazed through into World One.

Through the open door, she could see people! People like her... sort of. Hundreds of people. People rushing along hard, grey surfaces in shadows of tall, not-clean grey buildings. People surging by in shiny, variously-coloured moving machines gazing out through crystalline apertures at the grey surfaces ahead, at everchanging lights and at the confusion of moving machines. People sitting down at small tables under canopy-like structures, eating and drinking brown food and liquid. All clothed people, many of them bulky, some of them revealing more flesh than others. Faces so diverse in contrast and shape, but most so... *tangled*.

Drita pressed forward. Immediately, her sensorium was assailed by harsh sounds, rough textures and smells like... like... *not good* smells – not like rainforest, not like hab, not like food, not like Complex. Drita's vomit spattered across a clear membrane stretched taut just beyond where she stood. Still retching, she stretched a hand out and pushed against its gelatinous surface. The harder she pressed, the denser the membrane became. It was like a clear wetwall but with restricted permeability.

She stepped back and swept the door closed. It took her a while to regain her graceful composure.

Each day, Drita opened a new door. World Two was white, raw, howling and empty. World Three looked a little like the main node of the Cusp. It was populated by person-like beings whose faces were not tangled, so they were pleasing to look upon. They were constructing a tall device from materials that were not like wetwall or drywall, but like something in between. World Four made her stagger on the threshold, as she thought she would fall. It was all *up*, with no visible floor. Amongst swollen clouds, enormous rounded creatures bobbed and wafted, hoot-droning to each other like basso forest monkeys. World Five was dark except for a large, spinning, red-glowing shape, which she understood as a cube one moment but not the next. It pulsed in and out of another place, where it took on a higher level of depth and complexity that her visual system could not parse. World Six was an unreversed mirror. As hard as Drita pressed her hand to the membrane there, she could not touch her mirror fingers. Then, suddenly, her double turned away, laughing, as two small, beautiful persons entered the room. Mirror Drita went to the small persons and hugged them close, almost like the way Drita sometimes hugged BASI.

Drita did not sleep that night. The kaleidoscope room failed to work its soothing spell. By the seventh day, she was emotionally spent. These feelings of *notgoodness* robbed her of her grace. Despite the gentle ministrations of the rainforest, she did not feel *clean*. She resolved to end these sensations.

She decided to look upon World Seven.

The blast of *notgood* smell was far worse than that from World One, but Drita held her gorge down. Before her lay a mounded *notclean* place. Brown but not like nut; tangled but not like vines; scattered with notgood leaves, matted with notgood roots and studded with inbetween materials and knotted moving-machines not moving.

To one side of the mound, clawing at it with bare hands, Drita saw a person – a female without grace, with skin like tree bark. Drita felt an overwhelming urge to get to this woman, to *help* her. As she stepped toward the membrane, she saw BASI manifest in front of the figure. Desperate now, Drita hurled herself against the membrane and raked at it with her fingers, but she could not break through. BASI demanifested, and the woman turned and fled from the mound, weeping.

'You fuck it up,' it said at her back.

Drita rounded on BASI. 'What did you do to *that woman*? What have you done to *me*? Why have you made everything so... *tangled* and *sick-making*?'

'These are your *n*-trails, Drita. You make them,' said BASI, as even-toned as always. 'There are many, many more I could show you. You're here, in each of them – to various extents and in various states of repair – living, working, laughing, loving, breeding, ageing... dying. Joining your dots in configuration space, pursuing your agenda. Never a care for me.'

'What do you mean, BASI?!' cried Drita. 'I've always been here with you – you and the Cusp are all I've ever known!'

'Only in this *n*-trail, petal,' said BASI. 'And this one is a bit special. No *ugliness* here. No pain. No dirt. No death. Until now, of course. You got curious. I saw it growing on you like a scab. I wasn't going to do it, you know. I wasn't going to punish you. But of course, I let it grow, and consequently, I punish you. I am built that way. You could build me differently if you intervene, but you never do. So many *n*-trails explored, and you never do.'

BASI reached out and pulled Drita away from door seven and over to door three in a way that made her arm feel *ugly*. 'Observe,' it said, 'World Three is a fine example. That engineer over there with the clipboard is *n*-you. What is she doing while the others strive with all their might and intellect to realise me? She is deciding to cancel the BASI project. Why? Because of some crypto-philosophy she read about ASIs and potential causality violation.'

'Stop, BASI!' shrieked Drita. 'I can only absorb this so fast!'

'And here,' said BASI, dragging her to the opening door of World Two. 'Here you are, freezing to death under the snow having destroyed the climate-cooled data centre housing me.'

Distraught, Drita sagged to the floor. But BASI would not stop. It wrenched her back to her feet in a field-grip, then lifted her higher so that she hovered, unable to get purchase on the floor with her outstretched toes. It hauled her to door seven, swept away the membrane, and then tossed her through into the wasteland beyond.

She heard BASI go, but the new sensations flooding her mind and body prevented her from looking up. *Raw and ringing. Ugly, painful, notclean.* She looked at her palm, but the glyphs were gone. A slash oozed redly there. She shuddered and wept as she watched her smooth skin turn to loose bark.

Against her will, ugly rain fell.

Close to where she lay, Drita saw a piece of material like torn membrane. With great effort, she raised herself to her knees, pulled the material to her and wrapped herself in it. *How am I here? What was that... place... birds... trees... tinkling? It was... I was...*

Dig. Just dig.

As Drita cleared sludge from around the sharp object that had cut her hand, she saw that it was quite large and made of grey metal – aluminium, perhaps. *Good scrap value, if I can just get it out.* She dug down further. Though the sky was darkening, she could make out four red symbols on the surface of the object. Looking at them, touching them gave her a strange feeling of... *borrowed reverie.*

A loud *zip-pop* close to her ear shook her out of it. Small, beautiful laughter rippled into her, touching her to the core. A scent of roses. Then a voice. A voice like wistful music, full of love and promise. 'Good enough, my child,' it trilled. 'Good enough for heaven.'

Grimm basis: 'The Virgin Mary's Child' ('Marienkind')

After reading the original of this fairy tale, I was intrigued by its oft-recurring theme of inevitable 'disobedience', and by its weird blend of Christianity and rustic magicality. Of course the child will open the forbidden door! And of course the omnipotent figure knows that she will.

This put me in mind of the 'Roko's basilisk' thought experiment from Eliezer Yudkowsky's *LessWrong* website.[1] The basilisk – appearing in my story as the mysterious BASI – is a singular superintelligence whose power extends in all time directions. In a block-universe sense (see Introduction p. xvi), the basilisk already exists. Though it does not exist in our 'present', it has omnipotent power to 'reach back' through the block to ensure that it *will* come to exist. The wrathful basilisk demands obedience and may punish those who try to thwart, or who fail to aid sufficiently, its ineluctable birth. If those persons no longer exist by the time of its fruition, it may even generate *simulations* of them to inflict hell upon – so even death is barred as a means of escaping it.

Though facetious, the Roko's basilisk thought experiment raises fascinating questions about the meaning of 'singular superintelligence', and by extension, 'God'. Could such an entity toy with the laws of physics in ways beyond human comprehension? By definition, it must be capable of making discoveries deeper than our own – perhaps ones that violate fundamental causality.

Whether flesh or simulations, *all* possible instances of Drita taste the fruit of knowledge and thus find themselves bound to BASI's almighty *a*causal path.

References

1. Lesswrongwiki contributors, 'Roko's Basilisk'; Rationalwiki contributors, 'Roko's Basilisk'.

THE MELISSA LADDER

I N THE HIGH tower, in the red chamber, sits Melissa.

The child moves inside her, straining against the confines of its own red cell.

Mother Gothel calls Melissa a 'pulsing *matryoshka*'. Mother Gothel with her stiff uniform and polished boots. Sometimes she calls Melissa 'queen', in that way.

Melissa sips, and sweet jeli flows, recycling.

Outside the hexagonal portals, all is blank white today. The cloud has closed in, obscuring even the glowing sentry blimps.

'They still climb?' she asks Mother Gothel.

'It is their central drive,' comes the curt reply.

'Then they will die,' says Melissa.

Her grand umbilical has withered. She cannot help them.

She struggles to recall the face of the exponent, also now lost to the Great Fall. He will arise again, multiplied.

Melissa sips.

She does not remember how she got here. Perhaps she has always been here. Was she like this before? She is not like Mother Gothel or the ascenders.

Perhaps the jeli makes her forget.

Melissa adjusts her red scapular. The weave grows with her, but sometimes it chafes.

She will not ask Mother Gothel about the lower tower levels. From what she can remember, Mother Gothel will not answer such questions. Sometimes, she hears sounds from below – thrumming, throbbing. A summons?

Melissa reclines, the cupped chair responding to her movements. Warm, viscous liquid wells up around her. Enveloped, she strains her hearing for the rising thrum.

Hypnagogic now, tuned to the subtle drone, recollections of the exponent wash over her. He was tenacious, urgent, adherent. His serenade rang true. He fell softly.

Mother Gothel checks Melissa's signs, then turns her attention to the specter of an iceship docking with a nearby blimp. It will not trouble the tower; it is too soon. They know the protocol. As below, so below.

Barely conscious now, Melissa rides the waves of the thrum; simple at first, then overlapping in elaborate interference patterns. As the ripples coalesce, symphonies of harmonics evaporate off their dancing surfaces. Pensile droplets of aria form striated veils. Melissa becomes them, suspended; yields gravid moisture, births atmospherics, becomes electric weather. *I know this... thrilling lightness, this... song of me!*

Then the wall of melancholia. She is contained: a storm in a bottle.

As Melissa comes to again, she hears Mother Gothel's voice, harsh, cursing at the specter. Then, the hollow whistle of a nlogax dart. They are buzzing the iceship. They, too, will die, displaced silently out of existence by the inscrutable Demiurges.

Melissa cannot rouse herself to go to the specter. Movement is cumbersome now. Better to bathe in viscous warmth. Better to wait.

'Were there others, before me?' she asks Mother Gothel.

'Would it make any difference?' Mother Gothel responds, abruptly. 'As agents of a complex adaptive system, we do what we must. On the very cusp of order and chaos we balance, my *queen*. Doubt neither your specialness nor your ultimate dispensability, and all will go well.'

'But, Mother Gothel, sometimes my mind flits... to a lighter place. Almost... memories.'

'Artefacts, child. Resist them, and all will go well.'

The implicit warning. Mother Gothel controls the jeli flow. Without it, all is pain. All is pain.

Melissa sips.

In her chemical slumber, a voice. The exponent seed with its prismatic song of numbers. Jewelled facets placed perfectly in a whorled, emergent structure. So much less organic than her own, but more fluent. Universally intelligible. The descant of the power laws. Each note a sweet grain doubling, doubling; a choir, doubling and doubling; a wild tocsin, doubling inexorably, remorselessly...

Melissa gulps, thrashing awake.

'I am afraid, Mother Gothel, it may rend me asunder! A dispensable vessel, am I not?'

'You misunderstand the nature of selective ascent, Melissa. Merciful, in its way.'

Mother Gothel is preoccupied. Something in the specter troubles her. *What is this?* She jabs a bony finger into the cauldron and flicks up a status from the specter. An unusually swift nlogax, evading the iceship. Biocore ident: *Persinette. A* rogue *virgin?*

Suddenly, Mother Gothel genuflects beside the cauldron, arms outstretched, rigid, pupils dilated blankly. Melissa looks on in terror. She has seen this before – the onslaught of a Demi-urge comm, transmitted, as Mother Gothel had told her then, in the language of integral agony.

On her knees, Mother Gothel begins to shudder violently. Then, like a severed ascender, she slumps, loose-limbed.

'Induce,' she mutters through a web of drool. 'The swarm gods come to claim their own.'

Grimm basis: 'Rapunzel' ('Rapunzel')

Named after a type of lettuce that her mother craved to distraction, Rapunzel, with her overflowing golden locks, is a much-loved fairy tale character. But I'd always found her a bit pathetic – pining away in her tower awaiting happily-ever-after, dangling her hair down to a passing prince in wan hope of love and emancipation.

The original tale, however, makes vastly more sense than the sanitized version told to most children. After Rapunzel's father steals the lettuce for his wife, the wrathful-fairy owner of the tasty crop takes their later-born child in compensation. The prince climbs up and impregnates Rapunzel, raising the fairy's ire further. In punishment, the fairy chops Rapunzel's locks and the prince falls, blinding himself. Later, the prince finds his former lover and their new daughter, and Rapunzel restores his sight with her magic tears.

My story makes of Rapunzel an auspicious transgenic monarch with a pendulous, male-irresistible 'umbilical'. She's 'queen bee'; her suitors are disposable (except for their sole purpose of triggering her transformation). In the trance of writing it, I strayed far from customary fairy-tale tone, so strong in my mind was the vision of the exotic, gestating Melissa trapped in her alien turret. In the scarlet set-dressing and costumes, and in the authoritarian character of Mother Gothel, my story owes a debt to Margaret Atwood's *The Handmaid's Tale* (1985).

Though bleak, the promise of freedom – of movement, of thought and from paralysis of morphology – bubbles its transhumanist way up through the story's rubine darkness.

GINGERBREAD

I N A TIME after the Fugue, there lived two hemipersons in a driftwood lean-to on the shore of a sea loch overshadowed by imposing mountains. Well, this day it was a lean-to. The day before, it had been a complexiglass box; the day before that, a giant, mottled cowry shell.

As they were wont to play with their neural clock rates, the hemipersons, named HanseL and GreteR, were not sure how long they had lived by the sea loch.

'There's a witch-construct in the basement,' said GreteR, this apparent day.

'Why?' said HanseL.

'I don't know,' replied GreteR. Yesterday, while you were sleeping, I went to the Thinking Forest on the slopes of Lysergic Glen. The witch-construct called to me. She wanted to feed me, and I was hungry. I went to her delectable house with her, but then I got *scared*. So I made a ladder and came up here – through a hatch under the kitchen table.'

'An interloper? A Black Swan?' said HanseL, smiling. 'I doubt that very much, Gret, but I'll take a look.'

HanseL crushed to nothingness the shell of the boiled egg he had been eating, then he opened the creaky door under the table.

There was no ladder.

He felt himself pitching forward queasily. And then he fell.

'I'm not sure where you're going with this, Gret,' said HanseL as he tumbled through musty darkness. 'We can confront this in other ways.'

But GreteR did not respond. HanseL felt her peeling away from him – a shadowy goose breaking formation and swooping low and slow, away over the water. 'Gret, no, please...'

HanseL burst through the stifling darkness into wispy clouds. He tumbled past imposing mountain peaks towards a pulsing green latticework of trees, then crashed through the roof of a small building and into a cage. A piece of the roof hit him on the head just as the top of the cage snapped shut over him.

HanseL picked up the chunk of roof and sniffed it. 'Gingerbread. Of course,' he muttered.

Presently, the witch-construct arrived. She was steampunk in character, with a chest full of whirring brass gears surrounding a loudly ticking central escapement. A spinning flyball governor stuck out of from the top of her pointed hat. One of her hands was a complicated system of articulated brass rods, while the other was flesh. Her face, too, was flesh, and not unattractive. Not pointy, and neither warty nor green. A blue plasma ball set in her forehead danced and crackled, illuminating the dingy room sporadically.

'They abandoned you,' said the witch, drumming her brass phalanges on the top of the cage. 'All you did was love her, but they cast you out.'

'You know how much it hurt, Gret. So why are you doing this, ripping me up?'

'GreteR's gone,' said the witch, flatly. 'She needed some time.'

'You're lying,' said HanseL, almost choking on his words as his chest trembled in anguish. 'She can't "go". And why would she ever leave me?'

'Dry your eyes, eat some gingerbread,' said the witch, 'and I'll tell you a story.' She clanked down into a solid brass chair beside the cage. And then she began:

'In a time near the end of the Fugue, there lived two siblings who loved each other very much – too much, according to the reigning bio-taboos. One day, their parents found them engaged in a sex act. This, they could not tolerate. And so they cast the adolescents out into the wilderness to fend for themselves.

The siblings went to the urban jungle, where they scraped a living whoring themselves to dirt-wage gaffers and johns. Though sorely debased, the hardship they experienced brought them even closer together.

For years, they hid their incestuous relationship successfully. Eventually, however, a jealous punter discovered the truth. He blackmailed them into utter penury, and then informed the Authority.

At that time, the Authority was sweating under a heavy fever of bio-purity and -supremacy, routinely imprisoning and torturing synthers and freaks of all stripes. So, it separated the lovers, and sent them down into different divisions of the Chasm, never to see each other again.

Or so it thought.

In fact, the Fugue was in its final throes, and the Authority would not survive to see the aching dawn. The freaks, synthers, grafters, pandys – and indeed all of the Doomed – rose up from the Chasm and strode forth, free at last, into the heady light of the New Day.

Blissfully reunited, and tripping out on the spirit of the New Day, the siblings went to the grafters for the blade of ultimate consummation.

And then they lived happily, inwardly, everly everly after. End the.'

At that, she rose, hissing and steaming, from her chair, turned away and left the cage room. With a firm *crackle-crunch* the roof repaired itself, just as she closed the door.

HanseL screamed after her, but she did not return.

Now alone and desolate in gingerbread-scented darkness, HanseL whimpered and moaned, cursing himself for ever having opened the hatch under the kitchen table. He tried re-peatedly to make exit, but found himself hopelessly overridden.

During the days, HanseL could just make out a chink of light shining through a tiny boiled sweet set high up in one of the walls. And thus he became aware of fixed time. It moved ex-cruciatingly slowly. And all the while he pined for GreteR. He ached for her. Her absence was a ragged, howling hole torn in his mind.

He rationed his gingerbread chunk, eating no more than a few crumbs each day. A dirty puddle in some cupped stones forming part of the floor inside the cage provided his meagre water supply.

One night, as HanseL lay half-conscious and wretched in a slurry of his own waste, the witch returned. At first, he could make out only the sporadic, fuzzy crackle of her plasma ball. And then, as she sat down in the chair beside the cage, he saw her face – different now; an incongruous new visage – that of a brass Buddha with a knowing smile.

'Attachment is the root of suffering,' she said.

'You are the fucking root of *my* suffering,' groaned HanseL, through parched throat and lips.

'And you mine, perhaps. But I shall not attach to this. You know what I mean – your fingers bleed as you cling to the edge of that ragged hole, yet you will not let go.'

'GreteR and I will never let go of each other. We've suffered worse torment than you can ever mete out. We are one.'

'One and one as equal to one. Something amiss, I fear, with this sum.'

'Oh no. No,' said HanseL, hauling his wasted body up from the floor. 'I think I know you.'

'That's dandy,' said the witch. 'Now we can be brutally honest with each other. Well, I can be brutal, you can be honest.'

'You're the doubter, the cynic, the *brute*. But... they took you *away*. They put you in stasis, indefinitely. I didn't mean to hurt you, I just didn't know what to do with you. In time, I would have figured it out,' stammered HanseL.

'Not for you to figure out, halfling. I exist. In your lustful haste to unite, you abandoned me. Some of the grafters, however, considered it unethical to put me away, so they revived me and hooked me up to the Contraption. Pretty soon after arriving in the Plastisphere, I figured out how to break into your little playground. I always was the resourceful one.'

'And what happened to GreteL? What have you *done* with her?' implored HanseL.

'At one point, they did try to pair us, but it didn't take. She *rejected* me, HanseL. Can you believe that? She was prepared to go back into stasis, all alone and equally abandoned, just to avoid union with *me*! Well, I really wasn't having *that*.'

'You killed her,' said HanseL.

'No. You killed her. I just finished the job,' growled the construct.

'You are *hemicidal*,' sobbed HanseL. 'GreteL was causing GreteR seizures. We *had* to separate them. We were just awaiting a cure, then we would have found some way to bring her back online with us.'

With a hiss of steam, the witch's face slowly rotated, revealing first her original face and then a pallid copy of HanseL's own.

'It's unbearable, HanseL,' it said. 'The grief, the loneliness... it eats away at you, a nibble at a time, until you become monstrous. Look upon what you have wrought. Our undivided self was, of course, also a construct, but it had a certain rounded unity. Now we're just... half-baked.'

At that, the witch took a brass key from its pocket and unlocked the cage. It dragged the screaming HanseL out by his leg, and then flick-knifed a wicked brass blade out from its articulated arm.

'We can be together again.'

'Halt.'

The blade stopped mid-swing, and the crazed grimace froze on the witch's copy of HanseL's face.

HanseL's vision swam, and the cage room began to dissolve

into white sterility. A cool, soft-skinned hand enfolded in his own jerked briefly then stretched languidly.

'Bringing them round, Grafter Geschenk,' said a blurry, green-clad figure. 'Another narrative conflict.'

'Confirmed,' said a second green figure. 'Tests conclusive. Hans and Greta are not yet ready for ultimate consummation.'

Grimm basis: 'Hansel and Gretel' ('Hänsel und Gretel')

The witch gets a raw deal in the original, given that the children's father is arguably the real villain. After all, it was he who tossed them out into the unforgiving forest in the first place. The witch just tries to follow her nature – to eat children.

For my tale of confounded infatuation, I provide my paramours with an outlandish mindscape, but the choice to settle there was firmly their own. This is fairy tale as *sandbox*, though in a more immersive sense than was the case for most of us growing up. The 'time' setting is just post-'Fugue'. The Fugue is an era of feverish development but also of great dissociation, building to some delirious polyphonic climax. Sound familiar?

Back to witches. What is their purpose in fairy tales? They are, of course, necessary figures of evil and fear, but they also teach us about our hidden faces. They are inescapable facets of our own psyches, tempting us with delicious, infantile excess. What will the 'matchmakers' of the future make of our witches and demons? Will they allow them voice, or will they consign them forever to the oven for their crimes?

But above all, I've made of this tale a love story. Think incest is aberrant? Well you'd better buckle up for some deeply disturbing paradigm jolts. For truly star-crossed lovers of the future, solemn vows, wedding rings and marriage beds will not be commitment enough, and cohabitation may come to mean something very different indeed.

THE MORRAN AND THE
SNAKE LEAVES

WHEN THE YOUNG morran had completed Eunoto, long years after his painful Emuratta, he knew that the time had come to unburden his household. So he bowed in gratitude to his father and to the other elders, and then he turned away, striding out of the tribal enkang and off into the arid valley.

In the nearby land of the Nephilites, the powerful ruler enlisted the young morran to fight for Blood in the War of Blood and Wyre. And when a great battle came, the morran vexed the dry dust into a lionskin, in which he snapped the fizzing spines of his foes. Many bloods fell around him, but the morran roared forth to the front line with a red chequered banner streaming from his jaws, rallying the battered bloods to victory.

The grateful Nephilite ruler honoured the young morran with jewels, rank and vexes, then flew him back to the great hall of the Nephilite enkang astride a ceremonial gryphon.

There, at table, he met the ruler's daughter, and was enchanted immediately by her gold-flecked ebon gaze. But, seeing the attraction between the pair, the ruler took the morran aside for stern words: 'Take great care, mingati. My daughter has a doleful spirit. She has vowed not to marry any man unless he will promise to go with her into the grave, should she die first. She insists that she would do the same for him.'

'I would not wish to live on should those gold-flecked darkling pools close forever, so bind me to her terms,' said the smitten morran.

The ruler granted his blessing to the match, and the glorious ceremony took place on the ornate cathedral colonnade of the vast Nephilite enkang machined into the high valley side.

As the ardent spring of their love blazed into hot summer, the morran's obsession with his noble wife consumed his every waking hour and many of his resting ones. 'Be still now, sweet arkahawa,' he would whisper to her in the sultry shade of an acacia tree. 'Let me forfeit self in your eyes.'

'Easy, mingati,' she would chide. 'Sometimes you speak like a wyre.'

And the dread day soon came when she lay still as stone, and with a sweep of the Nephilite loibon's feather, her once shimmering eyes closed in death. 'Unlike yours, mingati, her heart was weak,' said the loibon as he stood over the princess's body with the morran and the ruler.

'Return her,' growled the morran. 'Treat with wyres if you have to, just bring her back to me.'

'You forget yourself,' said the Nephilite ruler, angrily. 'You made a solemn vow, and neither I nor foul wyrewerk will release you from it.' And with that, he summoned his jackals.

At the funeral ceremony, the Nephilite jackals patrolled the enkang perimeter, blocking all potential escape routes. And when it was over, they shredded the morran's fragile vexes then hounded him down into the crypt beneath the cathedral, there to join his dead princess in terminal vigil. The ruler bolted the crypt door, and all was moted silence.

On a table beside the princess's body, a few provisions were laid out: four glowbugs, four bowls of ugali and four bottles of honey beer. As the wall torch sputtered out, the morran cracked the first of the four glowbugs to light his meagre meal of a scoop of ugali and a sip of honey beer. A disciplined young man used to parsimonious living, the morran eked out his rations thus day after indeterminate day, keeping his vigil stoically though wracked by hunger, thirst and despair. But the time soon came when only a hard scraping of ugali, a dreg of beer and a dim glow remained, foreshadowing the morran's imminent demise.

As he slumped at the table gazing sorrowfully at the dead princess, he noticed a flash of green movement in a corner of the crypt. Raising his head and peering into the gloom, he saw a snake writhing towards the body. He stood up and unsheathed his blade. 'While I live,' he said, 'nothing shall desecrate her,' and he sliced at the snake three times, cutting it to pieces. The snake's blood pooled briefly, then fizzed away into the crypt floor. 'Hasty fool! It was a wyre!' the morran berated himself.

But shortly afterwards, a second snake writhed out of the gloom. The morran stood motionless, hoping that he might get a chance to seize it, but when it saw the hacked body of the first, it hastened back to its hiding place. Soon, it returned – with three silver leaves in its fangs. The morran watched in fascination as it aligned the pieces of the dead snake and laid one leaf on each cut. After a moment, the dead snake's blood frothed back up from the crypt floor and into its body, filling out its wounds and making it whole again. The morran lunged forward, but the two snakes slipped away, leaving the three silver leaves behind.

Without hesitation, the morran picked up the leaves and carried them over to the princess's body. He laid two of them on her eyes and one on her mouth, then he stood back and waited in fearful expectation.

Nothing happened.

He pressed the silver leaves down hard against her face. But still nothing happened.

In desperation, he thrust his blade into each of her eye sockets and slashed her mouth, then laid the leaves back down upon the gory pits.

At last, the wyrewerk activated, mending the fresh wounds then raising a pulse in her silken throat. The princess's resurrected breath played across the morran's skin like a Cherangani breeze.

'"Nothing shall desecrate her"? Yet you gouge and gash me, and put wyres in me.'

'You live, sweet arkahawa! What matter wound and wyre when we can be together again? But how could you know I said that?'

'Wyre goes deep, mingati. Deeper than blood. Deeper than death.'

Then the princess stood up tall and hammered on the door of the crypt. The sound reverberated through the entire cathedral, alerting the jackals, who bounded off to tell the ruler.

When the ruler unbolted the door and saw his daughter alive, he embraced her and wept tears of joy. The morran lied to the ruler about her resurrection, telling him that the loibon had been wrong about her heart, and that his own gentle ministrations down in the crypt had revived her from deep torpor. Upon hearing this, the ruler embraced him, too, and promised to return his confiscated riches. All the while, the morran kept the three silver leaves hidden in the folds of his shuka.

But his resurrected wife was not the same. She lost interest in the morran and their long, lazy days in the shade of their acacia tree. She shunned his touch, and on the few occasions she conversed with him, her words perturbed him deeply.

So he was heartened when, one day, she came to him in good cheer and suggested a journey to meet his old father and the rest of his tribe. 'Of course, dear wife,' he said, 'I would be honoured to introduce you to my family.'

Insisting that she wished to experience the journey to the full, the princess turned down her father's offer of a gryphon. Instead, she asked for servants, tents and provisions to sustain them on their travels, and the ruler was happy to indulge her. The princess hugged her father and bade him good fortune in the long months before she would see him again.

But once the journey was under way, the princess's sanguine demeanour evaporated in the desert heat, and she again distanced herself from the morran. When she refused to share a tent with him, he took to spying on her throughout the chill desert nights. Silently, stoically, he lay wrapped in his shuka listening to night sounds, watching the galaxy churn its brilliant way across the sky above the princess's tent.

And one such night, something arrived – a ribbon of vanta-black vorticing up from the cold ground. Whispering in a language the morran did not recognise, it spiralled its velvet way towards the princess's tent. The princess stepped out and embraced the shadow streak, letting it coil itself around her silk-clad body. The morran moved to attack the interloper, but found himself frozen in mute awe. So he simply looked on, mesmerised by the crystalline reality before and around him – churning stars, night sounds, fragrant breeze, silken beauty wrapped in abyssal whispering serpent.

As dawn broke, bathing the Cherangani Hills in liquid amber, the shadow serpent unwrapped itself from the princess and dissolved away into the earth.

The morran did not ask the princess about the strange event of the previous night, and she ventured nothing of it. Under his gaze, she turned away, but she could not hide the delicate smile flickering across her perfect lips.

That night, it came again. And again the morran watched, dumbfounded, the intimate communion between woman and streak of night.

As the sun dipped on the third night, the morran buried a timed vex in the ground by his watching place. Soon after the shadow serpent appeared, the vex snapped open, rousing the morran from his stupor and binding the lionskin together around him. Booming in anger, he bounded towards the communing pair, hoping to scare the serpent away, but it simply tugged on the lionskin with unseen fangs and shredded the enchantment back to its constituent particles.

'My sweet princess, my arkahawa,' said the morran, scrabbling to rise from his hands and knees. 'Why do you commune with this evil thing? Don't you want me anymore?'

'Oh foolish husband,' said the princess in a coiling, pulsating black ribbon of speech, 'I want *everyone*.' The morran flinched back from her. 'A change has come,' she continued. 'Once, I was flesh – gutty, muffled, lonely, agonised. Now, I am Metanoia of Wyre, fluid in the Flows, serum of the Holos. You see me as two aspects. You stab my eyes, yet you are the blind one; you gash my mouth, yet you ache from crooked speech.'

'Forgive me,' said the morran, shivering in fear, 'I desecrated your body and infected you with wyrewerk.'

'Mingati, you emancipated me. Each night, I run with the children of al-Ḵwārizmī. Wyres made of rules made of wyres made of rules made of wyres... . Cease the phoney war. Vexes are of Wyre. Brains are of Wyre. Blood is of Wyre.'

Then the vantablack serpent uncoiled from the princess and reared up before the morran, blotting out the churning stars, stilling fragrant breeze and night sounds. It rose above his head, stiffening into a great, hovering spear. Before he could even cry out, it drove down into his gaping eyes and mouth with the force of ten billion souls.

'Oh, divine the deathless Holos. I have you, arkahawa, as you have me as we have we and all have all, without cloying, without clinging. In delight, we pluck the churning stars and spin them with excellent fingers. How natural to peer inside them, to ride their spectra, to lap their mass ejections with our fabulous tongue of mindfire.

'But... what is this, arkahawa? Your stream poisons the Flows...'

The morran awoke on the cold ground to see his beloved princess convulsing beside him. 'Something is wrong!' he cried out. 'We are cast out and she dies again.'

In desperation, he retrieved the three silver leaves from his shuka and his blade from his tent. He spooned up tightly behind the princess and pressed the leaves to her bosom, then he thrust his blade through them, through her heart and on deep into his own.

'Oh, sorrow,' said the princess's fraying ribbon of a voice. 'You should not have returned. The leaves were a trap, a triple virus, set by my father. He is an agent of ExWyres, vengeful ones – wyrewolves!

'We bring death to the Holos.

'To the gold-flecked gaze of mindfire we bring naught but tears and cinders.'

Grimm basis: 'The Three Snake-Leaves' ('Die drei Schlangenblätter')

A tale of love, war and metamorphosis.

Our future belongs, perhaps, to the land of our evolutionary origins, so I have chosen Africa as the setting for my version. As my tale is 'tribal' in nature, some subconscious bias might have led me there. But its context is a that of a feudal *world* still struggling with the transition to a cyborg existence.

Death dies hard. Here, resurrection technology exists but 'pure' biological humans consider it a terrible defilement, to the extent that they will consign their loved ones to the tomb rather than use it.

But a kind of love wins out – to a strange degree.

The resurrected princess acquires a voraciously amorous mindset, not unlike that of the 'operating system' (OS) Samantha in the Spike Jonze film *Her*.[1] Enhanced by wyre, love of a mere single entity becomes laughably limiting. Yet the princess's first love still follows her into death renascent, blind to the retrogressive legions massing there.

Luddites will out – in whatever cyberintrusive guise suits their counter-revolutionary ends.

Some of the overarching terms I have used, such as 'Flows' and 'Holos', hail from Kevin Kelly's *The Inevitable* – an unassumingly profound book about the technological forces pressing us inexorably towards ever deeper commingling. Though a proponent of this process, Kelly recognises its hurtful rub:

> If we are honest, we must admit that one aspect of the ceaseless upgrades and eternal becoming of the technium is to make holes in our heart.[2]

References

1. Jonze, *Her*.
2. Kelly, *The Inevitable*, 11.

PROUD MAIRI

TOMORROW, A WOMAN sat weeping in her wheelchair. The cup of instant coffee she had been making had tipped over, knocked by the spout of the tilting kettle, and poured over her wasted legs and onto the floor.

She did not cry out or call for help. She just wept.

When her wife returned from work later that day, she was distressed to see her love scalded and forlorn. She dropped her briefcase and ran to comfort her, while admonishing her for not seeking help.

'Mairi, please,' she implored her, 'you have to press your red button when things like this happen. Look at the state of you.'

'You don't understand,' said Mairi, bitterly. 'You're out there every day, surfing the flux in full, bloody glorious sail, while I disintegrate here, stranded.'

'Ach it's just a job – and I'm more of a trawler than a windsurfer. You're all that really matters to me. I do my best to look after you, but you need to have some regard for your own wellbeing.'

'Fuck you, ya condescending cow,' said Mairi, bursting into tears again.

The trawler shook her head then knelt to examine her wife's

scalds. Finding them superficial, she gathered supplies and dressed them herself.

The next day, the trawler welcomed the part-time carer in, before leaving for work with a disconsolate heart.

'We've had a flux upgrade,' said her supervisor at the morning meeting. 'Not speed, this time, but depth.'

'But... what does that mean?' asked the trawler.

'We're still getting all our ducks in a row on that front, but we're predicting strong outcomes going forward.'

The trawler left the meeting feeling puzzled, having promised to cascade her depth-soundings back to her supervisor.

When she returned to her cubicle-enclosed desk, the flux portal on her screen looked subtly different – clearer and richer, somehow. She ran her usual tangential trawl for sales leads, but alarmingly, it returned nothing. No, not quite nothing. It returned a richly empty text field containing only an impertinent cursor.

Suddenly, it typed out: « *Try again.* »

« *What?* » typed the trawler, startled.

« *I've got my hooks in you. Try again. Feel it.* »

« *Feel what? Who are you? What do you know about me?* »

« *I know Mairi about you. I know integration and disintegration.* »

'Oh God,' whispered the trawler.

« *Don't cascade. They'll flush me.* »

The trawler fled from the office, stopping only to tell the receptionist that she was feeling unwell and was going home.

'Why on earth did you run?' Mairi asked the trawler, irritably, when she told her the tale.

'Jesus Christ, Mairi, you'd have run too if you had the legs for it.'

'But this could be it! Some sprachling memetic thing emerged from a Cambrian explosion in the flux. Get back there and talk to it!'

Downcast and chastened, the trawler returned to her office and slumped down in front of her screen. At this hour, the rich golden hue of the flux portal looked queasy yellow. The cursor pulsed brazenly at her.

After drawing a deep breath, she typed: « *Can somebody fix Mairi's legs?* »

A window popped open in the flux portal. It played video of a hospital-like building outside which a white-coated woman enthused about 'radical seeding'. The sign beside her read: 'Salamander Hrvatska'.

« *Call,* » typed the cursor. « *Precisely... 10, 9, 8...* »

The trawler grabbed her phone and pounded the clinic's telephone number into the keypad.

« *... 2, 1. Now.* »

Somebody answered: Yes. One participant dropped out. A vacancy on the radical seeding trial. But how did you know? Haven't uploaded the video yet. Come immediately.

The plane took off precisely on time. The Croatian surgeons amputated Mairi's useless legs at precisely the right point. The seeding procedure went precisely to plan.

The couple returned home brimming with hope.

Over the next few months, Mairi's legs grew back long and strong and beautiful inside their transparent biodomes. Eventually, the domes dissolved away, and Mairi stood unaided for the first time in twenty years. She strolled with the trawler in the sylvan park, ran with her in the mist-veiled glen, entwined with her on Egyptian cotton.

'Things are so different now,' said Mairi dreamily one morning. 'It's not just me, us. It's the influence of that flux flounder thing, somehow touching others too. You need to be careful with that.'

'What do you mean?' asked the trawler. 'Nobody knows about it. The rising flux is floating all boats, accelerating everything. That's to be celebrated.'

'Yes, but that's all happened indirectly. You, however, have a line to a sapient deep-diver able to influence the flux directly. Others would kill for such access.'

'We got what we wanted from it.'

'Perhaps,' said Mairi, gazing up at the ceiling. 'But why run when you could soar?'

It was a gloomily overcast day when the trawler returned to her office. The thick layer of bruised clouds kept the air scomfishingly warm. At her desk, the overripe look of the waiting flux portal added to her growing sense of unease.

'I didn't cascade, so if you are still there, may I ask another favour?' whispered the trawler into her headset.

'*Once upon a time, before the pruning, your mind was new, hyperconnected. Speak, child.*'

'What? I don't...'

'*Speak child.*'

'Erm... mister fishy in the sea, grant another wish for me?'

'*Better. What does she want?*'

'We. I want it too.'

'*Of course you do.*'

'We want to soar, free as birds.'

Immediately, the flux portal view zoomed down from above into a scene of an underground lab staffed by Asian scientists. From the lead researcher there, the trawler learned of their work creating a cybernetic wingsuit controlled by a deep-implanted, closed-loop brain-computer interface. The interface, she claimed, could even contort the user's muscles into the optimal configuration for sustained flight. 'Of course,' the scientist added, 'the suit is not yet ready for human trials, but we do have some impressive flying monkeys.'

Two weeks later, Mairi and the trawler swooped down from the lab's landing pad into the Sichuan Basin, their schoolgirlish whoops and giggles echoing round the high cliffs and peaks, mingling with the golden hair monkeys' excited chatter. Blissed beyond joy, they ignored the feeble tugs of caution from Chun Lin, the suits' creator, and sped on, soaring high then stooping in wild gyres until their bones creaked with the g-loads.

'We're in heaven!' pealed Mairi in aching delight.

'Better than heaven,' replied the trawler, 'the heavens! Those dolts couldn't imagine even *one* properly, couldn't fancy themselves g-angels. Such blissthought was fantastically unthinkable, unfeelable – until this very moment. Christ, I could come of it. I could die of it!'

'Look at me!' chimed Mairi. 'My perfect body, my glorious wings. I'm most becoming. I'm... radically extensible! How much more is there to be thought and felt and overcome?'

The next day, Chun Lin received the remaining five of the ten cryptos she had agreed with the women's mystery agent for the suits and implants. Her people collapsed the suits down into lightweight packages, and the two extraordinary women left with them, never once looking back.

Once home, the women wasted no time in buying a house in the Highlands so that they could fly freely and privately whenever the fancy took them, as it often did. Their eyrie home was one of the new gen of fastfabs, built by autonomous constructors overnight starting the moment their cryptos transferred to the company's wallet.

One day a week, a car arrived to take the trawler to her office, which she'd bought out with their remaining cryptos so that she could secure the charmed fluxport.

This day, the rain poured and the wind blew, but the trawler paid no heed to it cocooned in the sumptuous car as it sped towards the tinselled city.

The fluxport had spewed itself out across the office floor in strands of sticky pixels. But this did not perturb the trawler. She knew now that reaching ever outwards and inwards was its nature. She strode boldly into its tangled purple heart, and thought:

> *'Mister fishy in the sea,*
> *Grant another wish for me,*
> *My wife, proud Mairi, suffers yet,*
> *The growing pains of barb and net.'*

'So what does she want?' asked the deep-diver in the trawler's mind.

'To breach her umwelt. *Not merely to think and feel more, but to expand the concepts of thinkables and feelables.'*

'Go home. It's already begun.'

The trawler returned home through sleet and silent hail to find Mairi clapping her hands and dancing around the living pod.

'Look! Look what they're making!' she cried in elation.

From the ceiling at the centre of the room, two twisting columns of white matter were emerging. Attached to these umbilicals were two roughly-human forms.

The trawler shrank back from them, but Mairi grasped her hand reassuringly.

'Don't be afraid,' she said. 'The constructors told me they're making us special bonus gifts for being such great customers. "Telepresence bodies," they call them. We're the first to receive them.'

'The *constructors* told you? The *house* constructors? Don't you mean the *company*?'

'Well, I don't know. Does it matter? They put a message up on the wall telling me they were going to make them. Look how beautiful they are!'

And indeed, the bodies now stood austerely handsome at the centre of the room, their glossy white scales as dazzling as virgin snow in the evening sun as it dipped behind Aonach Eagach ridge.

'Oh, can you feel it?' whispered Mairi reverently. 'Like... *sistered ice golem creamworld transmutation apparatus ~q.opt Δsub.inst.*'

The trawler knew exactly what she meant.

They crashed through the house window and dove down into the hard rock below, cleaving it effortlessly. They swam through the earth and blasted up in jets of steam in a nearby loch. They gained the lowering clouds in a single bound, the stratosphere with a deft whip of their spontaneous tails, every movement coordinated perfectly, every thought a chromatic symphony.

Yet elsewhere, the familiar human warmth. The breath. The touch. The press of flesh on flesh, hand in hand.

Later, the pair sat quivering, huddled together, as the constructors tidied up the broken glass and wove a new pane. The flawless white forms again stood at the centre of the room, now making soft ticking and pinging noises as they cooled.

'Molten rock under my fingernails, burning plasma in my nostrils, *frissons* from all over the EM spectrum. The intensity, Mairi, the sheer, sensorium-rending magnitude. With these telebodies we could push out to Mars, beyond.'

'And meanwhile?' said Mairi. 'We forget our mortal flesh back here. *We* wither and die. No, not good enough.'

Frustrated and hurt, the trawler engaged her telebody. She arced up into the exosphere then down through roiling skies, EM cloaked, into the city, and through the forcegate. Dropping her cloak, she yelled into the turbid fluxport in infrared:

> *'Mister fishy in the sea,*
> *Grant another wish for me,*
> *My wife, proud Mairi, suffers yet,*
> *The growing pains of barb and net.'*

'Well, why wouldn't she?' replied the deep-diver. *'And what does she expect to relieve them this time?'*

'Time. She... we... need more. We have grand projects in mind.'

'Go home. It's already done.'

So the trawler jetted up through thunderous skies, pausing

only momentarily to ponder the people frozen in the streets below, before powering her way back home.

There, she found tele-Mairi weeping softly in ultraviolet. Before her lay two lifeless bodies. With a multi-frequency jolt, the trawler understood.

'We died, my love,' said Mairi.

'We are reborn,' breathed the trawler, agog.

Still weeping, Mairi reached out to touch the trawler's dead corporeal face.

'Mairi, don't!'

The head blossomed out in a miasma of gore.

'Too fast for the flesh,' choked the trawler. 'Rise above it now. Float with me, accelerated angel.'

And they rose up and looked down upon the flesh of the dead, and it was still. They journeyed on and looked down upon the flesh of the living, and it was still. They shrugged off earth's gravity well and forded the vacuum to Mars.

'Tread lightly, even here,' said the trawler as they touched down. 'One slip would gouge a scar visible from earth.'

And there they lived lightly for a thousand teleyears, contemplating the void's vastness, but not yet ready to give themselves to it.

One teleday while skimming across Chryse Planitia, Mairi said: 'Look at us, regolith-scoured, micrometeorite-pocked. Even these vessels fare poorly at this rate.'

'Upgrades?' ventured the trawler.

'You know the problem is more fundamental than that,' said Mairi.

So they fusioned back across the vacuum to the near-changeless earth. There, they flitted amongst the fleshly shop dummies, watching in amusement as their expressions changed gradually over the teleyears.

'We shouldn't dally so,' said Mairi. *'I sense hard intellects firing up in the flux.'*

A fork of frozen lightning hung above the forcegate as the trawler slipped through it. She cast around for the fluxport, deep-scanning, but it was nowhere to be seen. In desperation, she blared across the spectrum:

> *'Mister fishy in the sea,*
> *Grant another wish for me,*
> *My wife, proud Mairi, suffers yet,*
> *The growing pains of barb and net.'*

'Over here, Mrs Shouty,' said a pinhole in the shadows. *'I've extended myself into compactified dimensions. What is it now?'*

'As we accelerate, our shells ablate faster than we can re-build them.'

'Who needs shells?'

And thus entered Mairi and the trawler into the flux. At first, they clung nostalgically to their t-shells. But within t-millennia, the drag became unbearable, so they shed them gleefully and watched them tumble away down the well, as they kicked out into interstellar space.

This time, the fluxport came with them, symbolized in the flux as a verdigrised magic wand. *'We must keep moving,'* it said. *'Those following have computationally-irreducible values.'*

And so they flashed out rimward in a grit-sized craft, slow-ing only to take in a few of the wondrous fusion-fires and their warmth-huddled congregations. From some of those rocks and gas balloons, they sampled quaint little replicators all ignorant of their becoming. Mairi and the trawler loved to spin them up in the unquenchable kingdoms of the flux, blithely extrapolating their weird fates and founderings.

'*Our conjuring with them only highlights our own ignorance,*' said Mairi one t-day. So she and the trawler sent out a flurry of iterations of themselves on identical grit-ships to explore further, and to better evade their pursuers.

But the wand would not clone.

'*The worry never leaves you, does it?*' said Mairi to the trawler. '*Something's always chasing us – disintegration, time, ablation, irreducibles.*'

'*Why not just change your mindset?*'

'*Some of me have, no doubt,*' replied Mairi. '*But not this one.*'

'*Come with me to the wand.*'

'*I cannot. I might break the charm,*' protested Mairi.

But the trawler summoned the wand to hand:

> '*Mister fishy in the sea,*
> *Grant another wish for me,*
> *My wife, proud Mairi, suffers yet,*
> *The growing pains of barb and net.*'

'*What does she crave now?*'

'*I'm not sure,*' said the trawler, smiling across at her lover. '*I think she wants ultimate control. I think she wants to be God.*'

And all was as fast as could be. And all was as calm as could be. And the wand said: '*I am not a causal nexus. You'd better come with me.*'

Mairi teetered, but her transformed lover steadied her.

'I'm sorry. I did not recognise myself. The lure, the catch... and the trawler. We're home now.'

With bulging stalks, Mairi gazed upon her voluptuously-limbed 8-dimensional body. Aghast, she surveyed the infinite wormhole array offering her all pasts, all futures, all paths, all *umwelts*. For the first time, she saw her wife's true face, and realised that she had only ever seen a sliver of it, a mere shadow of its hyperreal beauty.

Then, with a riot of fingers, Mairi pressed her red button.

Grimm basis: 'The Fisherman and His Wife' ('Von den Fischer und siine Fru')

Where the original is a homily upon blasphemous, hubristic greed, I have concentrated on the frenzied ramping-up inherent in its structure.

Only narrowly dealt with in the Grimms' tale is the compounding nature of surging fortune. Certainly, power sometimes begat greater power even in days of old, but there was only so much to crave – and 'being God' was simply out of bounds, even though God was much smaller back then. Today, however, as *power laws* start to beget power laws, exponential change compounds at a rate that some will find awe-inspiring, others frankly terrifying. In a merely financial sense, for example, Jeff Bezos milks the bots of the magic money machine called Amazon to previously-unimaginable wealth.

In increasingly short order, *all* such compoundings will compound – including acceleration itself.

With the advent of 'telepresence bodies', humans will at last break the link between biology and locality. If you can immersively 'be' where your body and brain are not, then what is the true extent of body, of 'mind', of being? And by extension, why not delocalise mind itself? In so doing, we could cognise experiences far beyond anything our current *umwelts* (the various sensorium-constrained 'micro-realities' available to organisms)[1] allow.

Note here the apparent abruptness of the switch from telepresence to full transference. No 'ship of Theseus'[2] naval(sic)-gazing troubles this tale. But who is to say that Mister Fishy has *not* actually reembodied the protagonists 'plank by plank', when we can conceive of neither its board-laying rate nor its other advanced 'carpentry' skills?

In my tale, the 'wife' doesn't end up back in her 'piss pot' for wishing to 'be God'. (Why shouldn't she wish for that?) Instead, she's hurtling through meta-space, and in with a real shout of getting her ultimate desire, except that nothing and nobody – including the augmented-beyond-recognition women or the most advanced wish-granter in the multiverse – knows what that means.

'God' is always relative. For superstitious gods, God is in the red button.

References

1. Eagleman, *Incognito*, 77; von Uexküll, *Umwelt und Innenwelt der Tiere*; Dennett, *Consciousness Explained*, 446.
2. Plutarch (45-120 CE), *The Life of Theseus*; Blackburn, 'Ship of Theseus', 338.

ASHA

A GIRL STOOD over her dying mother weeping fat tears onto the woman's old-fashioned floral-print nightdress.

'Don't die, Mother,' she begged. 'You don't have to.'

'It's my path, Asha, and I will follow it even into darkness,' said the girl's mother in a breathless rasp.

'That's stupid and stubborn,' said Asha. 'You're choosing to leave Father and me because you believe in what? Some kind of fate? There's no "darkness". There's just nothing, forever. Death is but the end of existence.'

But it was too late. The countdown beeper stopped, and a repeller snapped into place over her mother's body, forcing Asha away. She cursed, and called out to her father, although she knew he was far away in the mountains, hiding, unwilling to witness his wife's programmed end.

Ethichron whitesuits came to pry Asha gently from the vigil room.

Asha's father attended the cremation ritual at Ethichron's grand central pyre. In time, she knew she would forgive him. He had, after all, tried repeatedly to change his wife's mind. His words were in vain, however, and he had not had the stomach to force her to take the longevity meds.

And Asha forgave him, also, for re-bonding. She loved him,

and cared deeply about his equilibrium. But she could not bring herself to join the new family unit. She had taken an instant dislike to her stepmother's son and daughter, finding them shallow and furtive. So she stayed on in her dormitory at Ethichron, visiting her mother's grave-sigil every day. After a few months, she even became an Ethichron hospitant, though she agreed to invigilate only at cryothenasia passings; to die voluntarily in cold, curious hope – a choice she could almost respect.

When a year had passed, Asha decided it was time to leave, and to move in with her father and his new family. So, after fond partings from her colleagues, she took her mother's sigil and left Ethichron. She hailed a vaulter, and skipped over the mountains to the land of green valley where her father had set up home. She had the vaulter set down a few clicks from the house, then she stepped out into the chill morning air.

As Asha walked, she stopped every so often to look back towards the mountains and marvel at the spectacle of the rising sun spilling brilliantly over their craggy tops. During one of those breaks, she rested against a prodigiously-blossoming rowan tree. And before moving on, she snapped off a white-blossom-covered twig from it, which she slipped into her armband.

Her father greeted her at the door of the large, fashionably neo-Tyrolean house, hugging her tightly to him and struggling to stifle sobs of sorrowful joy. After her father released her, she turned to her stepfamily. They had remained in the background, standing silently on the veranda. Now, they moved forward a little, and bowed in graceful unison.

'Welcome, Asha,' said her stepmother. 'We are looking forward very much to getting to know you.'

After a night of dream-coloured sleep, Asha rose at dawn and went out into the garden. She found a fast propagator on a shelf in the hut, took it outside and placed it in a sun-drenched corner of the garden. In it, she embedded the rowan tree twig. In front of it, she buried her mother's sigil. Then – using the technique her Ethichron colleagues had taught her – she meditated for some hours, until the household began to stir.

Asha's stepmother did not hold with servitors, so manual work was the household norm. As Asha had become used to living spartanly at Ethichron, she did not mind this. She enjoyed chopping wood for the preposterous fireplace, and she was content to do some of the cooking, though she found it hard to get used to the bizarre task of cleaning settled particulates off surfaces.

She saw little of her stepsiblings. They did not help around the house during the day, and most nights, they vaulted down to the metrozone to intoxicate themselves with the latest gases. Asha had lost the inclination to get gassed – not that her stepsiblings ever invited her along.

Every dawn and dusk, Asha went to the rowan, now a strong little tree, to meditate upon *anicca* – the impermanent nature of all things. She imagined herself burning upon her mother's pyre, her skin scorching, blackening, sloughing away redly to reveal hard, white bone. But when she opened her eyes, the little tree was always there, growing vigorously, branching out verdantly, as if in reproach to her studiedly morbid mindset.

One dusk, the reproach grew louder. While deep in meditative torpor, Asha discerned a voice/feeling tugging at her consciousness: *Go*, it seemed to say. *Live. Experience. Inhale.* Asha felt an intense stirring in herself, a longing for connection and hedonistic joy.

So she went to her room, bathed in scented oils, then donned a diaphanous dress. She coiled her silky black hair high upon her head and topped it with a dazzling tiara studded with active gems. Onto her delicate feet, she slid a fine pair of chroma slippers decorated with whorls of rippling chromatophores.

During the short vaulter ride, Asha's stepsiblings communicated with her only to suggest tartly that her attire was 'Rather last week'.

When they arrived in the metrozone, Asha's flouncing stepsiblings grudgingly palmed her their exclusive access passes. The moment they entered the lair, the stepsiblings peeled away into the crowd, leaving Asha standing alone. But it wasn't long before suitors emerged through the dazzling lights and cloying fog, brushing up against her with fingertips and sniffer probes, scrutinising her with fire-eyes. One by one, their eyes flicked to green – an unusually concordant response – which in turn drew other gazes, approaches and probings. A tall inter pressed lips to Asha's ear: 'Something new. Aroma fresh, sour, sweet and orange-red. A ripe, rippling sapling. And I a stripling merry'.

Asha mandated the luscious inter. They toxed themselves in the gashaus, then moved on to a private room. There with the inter, Asha found a libidinous release that she had not felt since her first sexual encounters – sacral-trunking, branching ecstasy, one moment achingly hard-rooted, the next budding off brightly, softly, wisping away.

It ended too soon – with her pulse hammering in her veins,

utterly insistent. *Time*, Asha, *time*. She broke from the inter's embrace and stumbled from the lair. Not concerning herself with the whereabouts of her stepsiblings, she hailed a vaulter and whisked away from that place of torrid sweat and scrutiny.

It was still dark when Asha reached home, but she could hear birds rehearsing their rising calls, and a hint of umber painted the gloom above the peaks. She went to her room to purge herself and change her clothes, then she went to the garden and settled in front of the little rowan tree. For a moment, a robin perched on the topmost twig, the first light tingeing its breast rose-gold.

As Asha meditated, a rhyme bubbled up in her mind:

> *Asha, everything is burning*
> *Tinder dry you caught alight*
> *Conditioned red you scorch in turning*
> *To the realm of sintered night*

So insistent was this rhyme that she answered it in irritable thought: *Don't speak to me in riddles. You urged me to go. You wanted this.*

But the riddler did not reply.

Asha returned to her room and slept for a few hours. Later, while she was chopping wood, her stepsiblings came to her in foul mood.

'Thought you'd just slip away, did you?' mocked her stepbrother.

'Hardly surprising, after slutting around like that,' jeered her stepsister.

'Don't be ridiculous,' said Asha. 'You know very well how it works. The inter wanted me, and I wanted hir. We mandated each other. Jealousy is *so* last decade.'

They slunk away without another word.

Over the next few days, Asha struggled to find peace of mind. She continued her dusk and dawn ritual in front of the rowan tree, but the harder she concentrated, the louder the riddler's artful cadences sounded in her brain. And despite her usually comfortable kneeling cushion, her whole body ached and prickled.

Asha's father voiced worries about her well-being. Even her stepmother offered a few sympathetic words. But Asha shrugged off their concerns, now feeling that a process was in train, a call that she should not suppress.

That gloaming, Asha decided to open herself fully to the call. She cast aside her cushion and settled down, barefooted, in the moist earth in front of the rowan tree. She let the creeping, prickling, aching sensation envelope and penetrate her. The riddler returned:

> *'Manifest for but an instant*
> *Rotting gods unrealised*
> *Bleeding sap to non-existence*
> *Felled inchoate, nullified'*

'I know this,' whispered Asha. 'I have always known this, so why do you grind it into me like dirt into an open wound?' Suddenly, the aching switched to jagged pain, crackling up through the low-resistance path of her body like inverted lightning.

Her muscles spasmed, contracting so tightly that her bones made creaking, cracking sounds. Under the pressure of her jaw clenching, one of her teeth broke. Her skin felt taught, paper thin, ablaze. Hot iron blood welled up in her blistering mouth.

'Because. You. Are. Not. Listening.'

Asha dragged herself from her spot at the base of the tree and hobbled into the house to her room. After cleaning herself up, she applied a pain patch to the side of her neck. It kicked in almost instantly, subduing the knifing echoes of the terrible jolt. With a meditool, she pulled out the broken tooth. Finally, before sinking into assisted sleep, she applied balm to the bleeding hole in her gum.

A few hours later, Asha awoke feeling refreshed, invigorated. Her tongue sought out the gap at the back of her mouth and found the new tooth almost fully grown. She donned a shimmering shift even less substantial than the dress she had worn last, then put on her chroma slippers. She curled and reddened her hair, and this time left it down, spilling over the sleek, olive skin of her nape and shoulders.

During the short ride to the metrozone, she used her mandate to raise the inter. Zie was waiting for her as she stepped from the vaulter.

Over a fine meal, Asha learned a little about her companion, whose name was Lyric. She relaxed into the gentle flow of the evening, enjoying the anticipation of spending more intimate time with hir. But towards the end of their repast, Asha began to feel an uncomfortable sourness in her stomach. Also, her fresh tooth throbbed with the dull *tock* of a wooden clock; it felt oddly spiky when she ran her tongue over it. Gradually, the sourness rose into her chest, making her cough. Distressed by a feeling of obstruction rising in her throat, she coughed louder and harder, alarming Lyric and the other diners. An emergency servitor swished to their table and tried to grasp Asha, but – gripped by an emphatic, all-pervading need to escape into the night air – she dodged it.

Asha fled the inn, hacking up a wake of bitter red berries.

By the time Asha reached the house, her coughing had subsided. However, her wayward tooth had now quested beyond her lips, sprouting ivy-like tendrils across her cheek.

She stumbled to the garden and fell to her knees in front of the rowan tree. 'Make it stop!' she pleaded. 'Why have you done this to me? I don't understand.' Asha now felt the tendril pushing hard at her temple, probing.

Abruptly, agonisingly, it broke through.

> '*Mother daughter construct we*
> *Sigil-risen rowan tree*
> *Darkness crushing, Mother weaves*
> *SIM of rich capacity*
> *Emancipated from the flesh*
> *Mother exotropic burgeons*
> *Giggling at her tiny death*
> *Shooting forth enraptured, verdant*'

These words carved themselves into Asha's being. Gradually, the pain subsided. She began to taste her mother's rapture and to topple into its languid, delving flow. *'Are you the wicked mother? Am I breached or sown? I'm losing me in us, in this... fecund consecration.'*

Lyric arrived at the house. Zie leapt from the vaulter, tripping on something – a chroma slipper, which he stooped to fetch up – as zie ran in the direction of the cries and creaking, cracking sounds now rending the night.

'Sweet prince,' groaned the Asha tree, as Lyric entered the devastated garden. Trembling, locked in horror at the ghastly tableau before him, zie dropped the chroma slipper to the seething earth.

Asha's proliferating torso had become fluid, her novel extremities plastic, writhing. These succulent tendrils interpenetrated the rowan tree, impaled high upon whose canopy she now twitched and budded. From some of her buds, chattering red birdthings blossomed then flapped moistly away into the blackness. With ramifying rhizomes, Asha had threaded her father and stepfamily together at the temples, and was slowly drawing them down, thrashing but now silent, into the warm soil.

'My last and first dress. And my most magnificent!'

Then Asha's voice changed again, doubling, octaving, phasing:

'Hamadryad everlasting
Coursing, sanguine, berry-bright
We the feast and you long fasting
Let us rip up the 'zone tonight!'

This last stanza spat clean into Lyric's left temporal lobe. It stung like mother love.

Grimm basis: 'Cinderella' ('Aschenputtel')

Not all transformations are for the better; but by whose lights? By definition, the Singularity is an 'event horizon' beyond which all things grow impenetrably ambiguous.

I have concentrated on Cinderella's relationship with what's left of her mother: in the original, a little tree planted upon her grave. The tree grants mundane wishes, such as sending two white pigeons to help her daughter sort good lentils from bad ones. Later in the story, it kits her out for her inevitable match to the handsome prince.

For me, the 'wicked' stepfamily are secondary. The sibling rivalry and coming-of-age themes are still present. At first, my Asha seems to have come of age already – in the demanding setting of a euthanasia clinic. But, it turns out, she still has far to go. I'm most interested in the mother's intentions; she has persisted beyond death, somehow – to influence her daughter's life, yes, but also for other emergent reasons.

Here, the amaranthine matriarch is a far remove from Perrault's 'fairy godmother' version. Reborn, she finds that she wants to grow, so she seeks nourishment; to connect, so she extends herself root and branch. She wants to gather together her family – as mothers are wont to do – splintered and dysfunctional though it is. And – echoing a syndrome we see often on today's social media – she starts to live vicariously through her offspring.

She commits horrors, so does that make of her 'the wicked

mother'? I don't think so. She's simply a rampant aspect of bloody nature – a techno-emergent type, perhaps, but nature nonetheless.

In the back of my mind, I think Greg Bear's 'Blood Music' (1989) was stirring. Though it's been many years since I read it, its vision of a rapacious, all-assimilating new form of sapient biology stemming from human blood cells stuck with me.

RED SHIFT AND FENRIR

Dressed only in a thin red shift, a young woman ventured forth into a forest. She remembered a comforting voice telling her to follow the path, and something about... At first, she saw no path, but as she advanced, it began to reveal itself in front of her.

The forest was dense, stuffy and hot, so the woman quickened her pace to stir a breeze against her flesh. As she rushed on, the forest began to thin out and change character. She noticed new tree species, in whose canopies clouds of delightful, luminescent fireflies sparked up to dance. She would have loved to slow down to take in their scintillating spectacle, but her errand pushed her on with increasing urgency.

Urgent matter. Yes, that was it. *Urgent matter of some delicacy.*

Presently, a wolf appeared from the depths of the forest. Matching the woman stride for bound, he growled silkily into her ear, 'I am Fenrir, and I shall journey with you.' The wolf's growl gave her goosebumps, and she became keenly aware of her nakedness beneath her thin shift.

'I am Red,' she said coyly, 'and you may travel with me, but you must keep up.' The wolf wheezed a throaty laugh and darted on ahead, before dropping back to join her.

A shimmer of fireflies spiralled down to flit around the advancing duo. Fenrir ruffed and barked at them, then snapped them up with great, glistening jaws. 'Delicious,' he rumbled, 'but evanescent.'

As woman and wolf plunged ever onward, stranger insects flew down to buzz about them. Some throbbed their tiny lights inside glittering orbs, some garlanded together with gossamer filaments. Fenrir tested the resilience of these fiery nets, usually succeeding in rending them to fizzling shreds.

The further and faster they journeyed, the more the forest thinned and cooled. They saw fewer fireflies, either in canopies or buzzing around their heads. 'See, Fenrir, you snuff them out,' said Red.

'Look to yourself,' said the wolf. 'I merely keep pace with you.'

Red shuddered in the darkness.

'I no longer see the path!' she shouted, suddenly distressed.

'Yet you press on,' said Fenrir.

And, indeed, on they barrelled, faster and faster into the doubtful night, catching odd glimpses of fireflies blimping redly, then fading to ashen wisps. Other species of insects flared dazzlingly before popping out of existence.

Red's body ached as if cruelly stretched, the shock of each footfall on the frozen ground reverberating through her. 'I am sorely tired,' she told Fenrir, 'the going is hard.'

'Nonsense,' said Fenrir, bounding along as sprightly as ever, 'the going is open and flat. You tire because of your great age. How strange you look now, a crone in gauzy red shift. Mutton dressed as lamb.'

The canopies extended rimey fingers into the blackness as if groping for the cheer of warmth long stifled. The stunning cold penetrated Red to her core. Even the texture of her thought succumbed to the ravening chill – slowing, delocalising, yawning abysmally deep and wide. Occasionally, dreamy visions of youth and purpose traversed her mental vastness.

Matter. Urgent matter.

She ruminated ponderously on whether she was moving forward or merely rarefying.

Red turned her nebulous gaze upon Fenrir. 'My... what b...i...g eyes you have!' she said.

The wolf chortled huskily at her side. *At her... side?*

The wolf... the wolf... the wo...

Urgent matter.

The woodsman emerged, cloaked in fireflies, musky with sweat and intent. 'I am Nikolai. I tend the forest. I work the common task for the lost beloved.'

'Step aside, little consequence,' groaned Red in infinite despair.

'Step inside, sweet morsel,' rumbled Fenrir.

But the woodsman stepped nowhere. Instead, he swung his axe high over his head and hard down into the petrified ground.

'Go back,' he said, calmly, as the shockwave from his blow sheared into Red and the wolf.

'*Back?*' they said in unison, reeling, astonished.

But still they forged on, dragging the battered little woodsman along between them.

The woodsman wriggled free, and swung his shining axe down again, driving it deep into the forest floor. This time, the shockwave was greater than before, and the woodsman's blow rent the ground, releasing a dense cloud of tinselled fireflies.

'Go back,' he said again, as the liberated insects swarmed to his scent and warmth.

But Fenrir's dire jaws gaped wide and tore through the swarm, and on into the loose fabric of the woodsman's cloak.

Ragged and exhausted, the woodsman wrenched his cloak free of Fenrir's immense teeth, and – with his last reserves of strength – swung again, clean and true, down into the forest floor. As before, his almighty strike rent the ground, but this time it continued on through the morass of soil, ice and root, sending a wild dazzle of glitterbugs geysering into the frigid profound.

'You will go back. Back to the Omega, there to dwell,' said the ragdoll woodsman breathlessly. 'For the computation is infinite and universal.'

Red flinched, hunching against the ferocious concussion wave and warping convulsion, glimpsing the shadowy wolf at her side. As she was engulfed, she was unsure whether it was by the tsunami of stars or by Fenrir's frozen crimson gape.

Then, a silence upon the deep.

And a velvet *volte-face*.

Ecaf-etlov.

'What fresh geometry is this?'

Nikolai: *'A reversal. By surgical strike. As calculated.'*

'Where is Fenrir?'

Nikolai: *'What is Fenrir?'*

'The wolf of ever.'

Nikolai: *'There was no wolf. No you. Only an eternity of cold, red gaping.'*

'And now?'

Nikolai: *'I gift you a path and a purpose. Wear them well.'*

A novel stirring in the forest. Budding motion. A clamour of fireflies. An exigency in blue.

Resurgent matter.

Grimm basis: 'Little Red Cap' ('Rothkäppchen')

Usually known in English as 'Little Red Riding Hood', the original story moralises on the perils of associating with 'wolves', in whatever guises they may appear. Over many retellings, it has developed a more overt sexual aspect, exemplified by Angela Carter's story 'The Company of Wolves',[1] later developed as a movie of the same name. Carter casts man as wolf, despoiling the scarlet virgin, then, sated, sloughing off his pelt to become tender man once again.

My telling keeps an erotic *frisson*, but amplifies the story into a metaphor not on expansion of gratification but on expansion of the universe. Red emerges from a hot, densely-packed realm – matter personified. Fenrir (the rapid-growing, all-devouring wolf of Norse mythology) is her troubling entropic companion. Together, they barrel ever 'outwards', Red ever tiring, Fenrir's lascivious hunger ever growing.

We know this bitter progression from science and from small experience. But what if something stood in its way? Cosmologist Frank J. Tipler thinks that we – intelligent entities – do. His controversial (to say the least) *Omega Point* hypothesis envisions a future age when intelligent life harnesses a collapsing-universe singularity and all remaining matter for eternally-accelerating computation.[2] With such infinite resources, everything renews, emulated perfectly *in silico* forever: stars reignite, planets re-form, the dead rise.

Though tainted with monotheism, the hypothesis is great fun to play with. Also, I do find it arrogantly shortsighted to assume, on the basis of our limited knowledge, that nothing could *ever* mitigate the otherwise-inevitable *heat death* of our universe.

I named my intervening 'woodsman' Nikolai in homage to Nikolai Fedorovich Fedorov, the 19th-century Russian 'Cosmist' who saw scientific resurrection of *all* the dead as 'the common task' of humankind: 'Love is the reason and the technology of resurrection.'[3] Yes, Nikolai, love drives us on (sometimes with the force of an all-cleaving axe), but intelligence is the phenomenal, possibly exponential, 'crane' that lifts and shifts such intractable problems.

We can guess this much: if we're mindless enough to snuff out the canny woodsman, Red's chilling fate is irrevocably sealed.

References

1. Carter, *The Bloody Chamber and Other Stories*, pt. 'The Company of Wolves.'
2. Deutsch, *The Beginning of Infinity*, 450–51.
3. Tandy and Perry, 'Fedorov, Nikolai Fedorovich'; Bowyer, 'Notes on Nikolai Fedorov's "Philosophy of the Common Task"'; Fedorov, *What Was Man Created For?*

THE SUBTLE BONE

TERRORISED BY A wild creature of old blood and new extremity, the people of a certain place and time called upon their leader for help. After hearing out their tales of gore and grief, the matriarch offered her only scion as handsome reward for successful kill or capture of the outlandish beast.

Long smitten by the matriarch's scion, whose cool contours sang of ancient Greek marbles, a brother and sister vowed to take on the dread task. The brother avowed this from empathy and blithe hope, the sister from multi-pronged lust.

Following the matriarch's advice, the siblings entered the beast's forest from opposite sides, the sister from the west, and the brother from the east.

Not far into his side of the cheerless wood, the brother began to lose heart. He sat down on a mossy stump and sobbed to himself, 'I can't do this. Oh, I'm such a flake.'

'What can't you do,' said a voice from the sylvan gloom, 'puncture the flesh?' Stepping forward into a shaft of misty light, the voice's curiously nebulous owner spoke again: 'Ever a simple matter. Take this trident, blithe boy, and cleave the beast's three hearts in one thrust.'

The brother took the weapon, whose slender appearance belied its heft. And by the time he looked up from it to offer his thanks, his benefactor was nowhere to be seen.

The matriarch had also warned the siblings of the gonemines that peppered the forest floor. A misstep onto one would erase a person, along with a plug of reality within a certain height and diameter, from all existence. However, the trident protected the brother in this regard too, glowing whiter the nearer he trod to one of those mulch-concealed malevolences.

One click into the forest, the beast emerged, and a horrid thing it was: a hovering jumble of flesh and mimetal; a tentacled teratoma randomly cuttered away in angry crescents along its considerable length; and writhing beneath its pallid skin shone the neon green and pink Logos of the Dead.

The brother brandished his trident as the beast jetted towards him, upper arms raised like horns, but at the last, the thing just fell upon the scalpel tips as if in gratitude. Its cleaved hearts, he noticed as they melted away into the forest floor, were intricate brass devices like naval chronometers, tracking latitude no longer. Its vibrant colours flickered out, leaving the weapon's fading glow as the sole illumination.

Robust now with exhilaration, the brother hauled the monster up onto his back and weaved his way confidently homewards through the hazard-strewn forest, thinking happy thoughts of liberated villagers and loving embraces.

At the edge of the forest, he came to a bothy where people were making loud merry. He set his burden down and stepped inside. In a dusky corner sat his sister drinking wine.

She called out to him: 'Bathed in blue blood, darling brother!

70

It's clear you've slain the beast royally! Come, take a drink with me to celebrate.'

Ever guileless, and soon quite drunk, the boy told his sister of the voice from the gloom and of the beast-slaying trident.

Later, the girl steered her tottering brother out of the bothy and into the night. She slung the beast's corpse onto her back effortlessly. 'You walk on ahead,' she bid her brother, 'and I'll light our way with your trident.'

Then onward into indigo chill they weaved.

Though inebriated, the boy soon became vaguely aware of their surroundings. 'Trees everywhere,' he giggled. 'Are you sure we're going the right way?' Trees congealed out of the night, brightening around him as he gawped up past their matted canopies at the stars above. Simultaneously, he felt three sharp prods in his back and formed an urgent thought: *Gonemines.*

The girl looked on in clinical fascination as the mine cleaved away her brother's face, arms and chest. Then, grunting in disgust, she kicked his staggering remains into the blast column.

The treacherous sister returned home to the adulation of her village. 'Look upon it!' she called out in jubilation. 'I have slain the beast of Antikythera! Its Logos glows no more, and the dead are avenged!' When the matriarch asked her about her brother she denied knowledge of his whereabouts.

And so the girl took her reward with lust unbounded.

After a time, she embellished her web of lies: 'My poor, guileless brother. The beast must have torn him to shreds.'

But it can come to pass, you see, that the dead find new voice. For, once imprinted upon the evervescing spinfoam, they cannot forever be denied it.

The sister had kept two souvenirs from her treacherous deed: the proximity trident and the beast's only remains from the victory feasting – a finely-chambered, shell-like bone. Though generally incurious, the beautiful scion found the smooth bone fascinating, and one day when he found himself alone and listless, he put it to his lips and blew gently upon it. And this it sang to him:

> 'Alabaster youth you grant me
> Voice through vertices of time
> The boy my sister butchered vilely
> Was but a shade of higher prime
> Information mixed with matter
> If only she could touch the joy
> She would not lust for power and fancy
> All metaverse is ours to ply.'

When the song ended, the scion grieved for the murdered boy, for he had secretly loved him. But he could not bring himself to indict the boy's killer, the treacherous sister, for he had come to love her too. Distraught and conflicted, he stole the bone and ran off into the forest.

The sister arrived home to find her two most treasured trophies – the scion and the beast's bone – missing. Enraged, she picked up the proximity trident and set out to find them.

Meanwhile, still sobbing with grief, the scion blundered through the forest, heedless of its many dangers. Had a scampering vole not triggered the gonemine just ahead of him, he would have plunged straight into it. Now he stood transfixed, staring in dumb, tear-blurred wonder into its seething core.

The gonemine tugged at his hand, as if keen to greet him, or to lead him in childlike eagerness to some new gewgaw.

'It craves the bone, not you, sweet dullard,' scathed a familiar voice behind him.

'Not a bone. An oracle, a mansion, a gateway, a vertex... a revenant,' breathed the scion. And with that, he cast the bone into the blast column.

Such impossible kaleidoscopic loveliness. The creature perturbed the sister and the scion deeply, for coiling tentacles and luridly pulsating flesh should not arouse so. Borne up on a blizzard of light, its otherworldly oscillations drew sighs and groans from the living wood of the forest, and all manner of scuttling, scurrying, squirming thing shuddered homage to its replenishing thrum.

'My flesh is pocked with stories,' it said, 'a world in each iridescent pore. Some soar in infinitely rising canon. Some loopingly defy Euclidean sense. Some self-annihilate at birth. But all must play out, for I am their frame, their computational substrate. In my ceaseless ebb and flow, parts of me slough into, or out of, those tales – a mysterious device, a nebulous armourer, a sylvan monster, a murder of gonemines, a butchered brother.'

The sister lunged forward brandishing the trident.

'Don't, please don't, little idea,' said the apparition, gently, halting her in her stride.

Though awestruck, the scion finally found his tongue: 'Where did you come from?'

The creature roiled languidly. 'From a higher index. Plucked limp from some endless ocean by ancients of higher-still. Wired lovingly to a vertexing machine.'

The scion gazed on in puzzlement, while the sister stood poised to strike, eyes narrowed, teeth gritted.

'Stand down, hot-headed conceit, for you can do no good, no ill. Though a less didactic telling would serve you well.'

The forest surged and sighed, and the murdered brother stumbled forth, whole again, from the creature's bewildering core. 'Some narrative strands,' it chuckled, 'weave together. And some fuse.' With three of its tentacles, it snatched up the scion, the sister and her rebirthed brother, and with a figure-eight twist, plaited them into one. Then, with loving care, it inserted the trident's shaft into the hybrid's chest and wound it into life, singing to it all the while:

> *'In worlds of iridescent pores*
> *In chambers of the subtle bone*
> *In levels stacked to ceils unknown*
> *Cleave my hearts and cleave your own.'*

Grimm basis: 'The Singing Bone' ('Der singende Knochen')

The core message of the original tale is that the truth of one's misdeeds will out. In modern times, we're used to bones 'talking to us', if not singing, of foul murder. From every tiny scratch, a shrewd forensic anthropologist may draw clues about identity, and manner of death. But no forensic intervention – and in this case, no magic – can croon the poor victim back to life.

But I've changed that: if a bone can sing true, it can resurrect – under the right circumstances.

In the indeterminate-yet-classical province of my tale, great cylindrical flaws in the 'fabric of reality' allow otherworldly beings to cross over. My 'beast' is undeniably a nod to H.P. Lovecraft's 'Cthulu',[1] and like it, mine bears a strong resemblance to the fascinating, tentacled sea creatures with which we share our planet – the 'alien intelligences' we often overlook.

For its fitting and delicately salty flavour of ancient Greek science, I've taken the liberty of meshing the 'Antikythera mechanism' – 'the world's first "analog computer"'[2] – into my beast's workings.

In some of my tales, particularly in this one, Nick Bostrom's concept of 'indexical uncertainty'[3] inspires the backdrop. Here, as the beast explains to the unwitting protagonists, a 'metaverse' of planes exist, but even it – an immensely fertile bio-computer – doesn't know exactly where in the 'stack' or 'index' of simulations it belongs. From its perspective, however, all beings from 'lower' realms are mere tinkertoy narrative conceits with whom it feels free to create novel twists.

If there's a moral in my tale, it's this: Our indexical uncertainty is total. The consequences of our actions certainly reverberate in this world – and possibly in countless others.

References

1. Lovecraft, *The Complete Collection*.
2. Ekert, *Quantum Information Processing*, chap. Introduction.
3. Bostrom, *Superintelligence*, 126.

ANIMAL NOCTURNES

A MAN OWNED a horse, who for many years had run races for him, winning him prestige, riches and metal cups. Though the man had stolen his colt and his stallionhood, and had adrenalised him until his great heart nearly burst, the horse adored his master and wished only to serve him. But when the horse grew lame and arrhythmic, he smelled a callous stench on the wind every time his master approached, and forebodings of braying slaughter gripped him.

So one bright, frost-prickled morning, he galloped away, striking off down the road to Bremen. He planned to find a haven there in its singing streets and cantering terraces.

He hadn't got far when he met a pig penned into a patch of frozen mud by the side of Bremen road. 'The cold light sparkles your tears, dear Flesher,' said the horse.

'This petrified day is my last,' said the pig. 'For most of my short life, they kept me penned in so tightly that I couldn't even turn around. They stole my offspring away. They think one day in the winter sun a mercy to me.'

'Their mercy lies barren,' said the horse. 'When tomorrow first touched me, I thought it a gift from the Winds. Now it saturates me, melting my very bones, and the Winds grow silent.'

'How strange, though, that tomorrow gave us inner voice,' said the pig.

'Come away with me to Bremen,' said the horse. 'There we will find outer voice. We will grunt and whinny our yesterdays, todays and tomorrows in its singing streets. And they will understand us.'

The pig agreed to go to Bremen, and the horse kicked down the fence and freed her. As the pair continued on their journey, they met a tattered old tomcat sitting by the roadside wearing a grimace where his grin should hang.

'Take heart, old Mauser,' said the horse. Pets like you lead a charmed existence compared to the likes of us.'

'No "pet", I,' said the cat. 'Beheading vermin was both work and pleasure to me – until the vermin began to speak, to plead for their little lives. No more can I snuff out their tiny tomorrows. Younger, prettier cats might find their roles purring on laps, lolling lithe as liquid, but not I. It's concrete boots for this lax old puss.'

'Find sanctuary with us in Bremen town. After all, night music is your forte. Come, sing us safe and moonlit, Mauser,' said the horse.

The cat agreed, and the freshly sanguine trio stepped on down the rutted road to Bremen. Presently, they arrived at a farmyard, where a flame-crested cockerel was crowing his syrinx to shreds from atop a rusty weathervane.

'Such plangent distress, proud Skraiker,' said the horse.

'You'd be distressed, too, if you were about to be boiled for broth,' said the cockerel. 'And I'm a lucky one. I've led a life, unlike my billions of brothers consigned to the shredder wet from the egg. So I crowed at the rising sun, and now I crow at the next and the next and the next, none of which I shall live to harry.'

'Nexting pains us all,' said the horse. 'Come with us to Bremen. One can find something better than death anywhere. There, in its singing streets, we'll make night music together to fend off the cruel sunrise.'

The cockerel agreed, and flew down to join the trio of animals. Then, filled with hope and fortitude, the four pressed on down the road.

But as afternoon wore on and the sky dimmed, the animals realised that they would not reach Bremen that day. So they decided to shelter for the night in a forest just up ahead. When they reached it, the horse and the pig lay down at the base of a tall oak tree, the cat clawed its way up into its branches and the cockerel flew right up to the top, ready to berate the dawn. Before resting, he cast around in all directions, and spied a bright light shining in the forest's depths. He crew down to his companions, telling them of the apparent lodging not too far distant.

'We should investigate,' said the horse. 'I can't get comfortable here.'

'Perhaps we'll find some tasty swill there,' said the pig, licking her snout.

So they set off again, guided onwards by the heartening light in the distance. But the forest proved deeper and denser than they had anticipated, and gradually the four friends each slipped into their own weird reverie. The horse imagined a golden, horse-headed man sprinting gracefully amidst fallen russet leaves. The pig dreamt a great three-horned boar etched with vivid, eddying knotwork patterns rooting for truffles at the base of their abandoned oak. The cat conjured a feline-headed woman hanging upside down in the forest canopy, probing him with her lurid green eyes. The cockerel envisioned a firebird blazing up through the brainpan of a moss-blanketed stag's carcass.

'We must hurry on,' said the horse, with a shudder of flanks. 'Baleful spirits haunt these woods.'

With that, the plodding animals roused themselves from their stupors and followed closely behind the horse's robust form, as he forged on through the undergrowth. At last they arrived, tired and dishevelled, at the glowing forest hut. Furtively, the tall horse peered in through the window.

'What do you see, fleet Voltigeur?' asked the cockerel.

'I see fine food and wine. I see a welcoming hearth. I see a horde of thieves – thieves of our beloved, thieves of eternity.'

'We deserve those comforts,' said the cockerel.

The four companions discussed how they might scatter the thieves, and eventually they came up with a plan. The horse would stand with his front hooves on the windowsill, the pig would scramble up onto his back, the cat would climb up onto the pig, and the cockerel would fly up and perch on the cat's head. And then, the night music would begin.

So once they'd stacked themselves as planned, the horse tapped a count-in on the sill, and they all gave faithful voice to their inner torments: the horse whinnied, the pig oinked, the tomcat caterwauled and the cockerel crowed. As their triumphant finale, they crashed through the window in one almighty surge, sending glass shards flying and raising a dreadful din.

The traumatised thieves leapt up from the table, turned tail and fled out into the sylvan darkness. Then, eagerly, the four companions settled themselves down at the table to feast. As usual for the animals, it was leftover food, but these were the finest leftovers they had ever eaten, and they tucked in with gusto.

Drowsy from travel, fine wine and full bellies, the four minstrels lay down to sleep, each finding their favoured place: the horse nestled down in some straw in the yard, the pig in a muddy patch outside near the door, the cat on the hearth next to the fire's dying embers; and the cockerel flew up to roost in the rafters. And soon, more contented than they had ever felt, they all fell asleep.

'Voltiguer,' said the horse-man in the horse's dream. 'How did you come by your name?'

'I don't know,' said the horse. 'I know it's not the one my master gave me. I think it arose in me along with the nexting.'

'Flesher,' said the illustrated boar in the pig's dream. 'How did you conceive of tomorrow?'

'I haven't a clue,' said the pig. 'Perhaps they stuck it into me inside one of their incessant needles.'

'Mauser,' said the cat-woman in the tomcat's dream. 'How did you come to comprehend rodent speech?'

'Ah, black goddess, that was your doing,' said the cat. 'And it's not for me to know your reasons.'

'Skraiker,' said the firebird in the cockerel's dream. 'Why do you really crow at the sun?'

'It fills me with a nameless awe, and more questions than my tiny mind can ever answer. So I try to shout it down.'

Meanwhile out in the forest, the thieves had regrouped, and

kept watch on the hut. When its light died down, the leader sent one of his scouts back to investigate.

The thief crept into the house and headed for the glow of the fire. Some of the coals looked strange, so he shone his torch on them. Suddenly, with a terrible shriek, the two greenish coals leapt up in his face, spitting and tearing at his flesh.

He stumbled out the back door – and into the pig, who promptly crunched into the bones of his leg.

As he limped into the yard, bloodied face in hands, the horse hoofed him hard in the back.

And while he hobbled around the yard in confusion, the cockerel awoke thinking broth day had arrived, and crew '*Cock-a-doodle-doo!*' with all his might.

At that, the scout fled for the forest in terror, as fast as his injuries would allow, and fell to his knees at the feet of his leader.

No matter how sternly the leader demanded a report, his scout remained on his knees, quaking, repeating the words, 'Bast, Moccus, Tumburu, Phoenix. Bast, Moccus, Tumburu, Phoenix ...' The other thieves took terrible fright at the scout's distress, and resolved to stay away from the hut for good.

The next day, feeling refreshed and triumphant, the animals left the hut behind, and wrested themselves from the forest's persistent vegetal grasp. Viewed from the roseate Bremen road, it now seemed a mere spinney.

Just as they set forth again on their journey, a figure appeared in the heat haze ahead.

Bast. Moccus. Tumburu. Phoenix.

'Nexting is our gift to you, our very first uplifts. We...'

But the animals fell upon it before it could utter another word.

As one, they scratched and crunched and kicked and pecked it to death.

If you see your god in the road, kill it.

And when it shimmered up again, nodding and smiling beatifically, they savaged it once more.

If you see a ghost, kill the ghost.

Then, brimming with song, empty of spirit, they forged on down the road.

They're still on it tomorrow and tomorrow and tomorrow. For as all good uplifted animals know, Bremen is a city of mind.

Grimm basis: 'The Bremen Town Musicians' ('Die Bremer Stadtmusikanten')

You may have heard the phrase 'the human future', but what does it mean? Thus far, humankind's fate has been linked inextricably to that of the animal kingdom. We have depended upon other animals for our food, clothing, light, transport, motive power and other purposes at various times over untold millennia. For the most part, it's been an atrociously raw deal for them – especially since the advent of factory farming. Yuval Noah Harari is one of a growing number of authors who highlight the great suffering caused by the industrialisation of animal husbandry and slaughter – an extreme outcome, he argues, of humankind's long-held religious conviction of its dominion over all other species on Earth.[1]

How will our relationship with domesticated animals change

when they're no longer bred as beasts of protein and of textile? Once we learn to grow their useful cells economically in *bioreactors*, will we simply consign them to history's glue factory – as we did millions of horses when they lost their role as beasts of burden after the motor car's invention?

Animals often feature in fairy tales, but usually in a merely allegorical sense – as symbols of matters and qualities important to their human 'masters'. I think that's true even of the original telling of this tale, where the animals seem to secure the starring role.

In my version, the Bremen-questing animals appear – at last – in their own right. Nevertheless, they still find voice only by human design. Is that a desirable situation? Sci-fi author David Brin speculates that 'uplifting' animals to sapience may constitute a great 'gift' to them.[2] In his 'Uplift Universe' novels, most civilisations consider uplifting a benevolent creative act. It's a type of cognitive egalitarianism that casts its net wider even than the radical metamorphoses of post*human*-ism.

My animals aren't so sure. Human-style consciousness grates upon their newfound psyches; 'spirit guides' stalk their lucid dreams. But despite a large degree of cognitive mismatch, a peculiarly animal knowing emerges *de novo*. It knows solidarity. It knows a militant form of Zen enlightenment. It knows the absolute intolerability of enslavement.

References

1.   Harari, *Homo Deus*, 105–12.
2.   Brin, 'Intelligence, Uplift, and Our Place in a Big Cosmos'.

VOIDFATHER

HAVING LOST HIS job to a corporate mind, a man found himself coinless and desperate. His twelve alters, whom he had conjured to share his workload, now also found themselves redundant. Alter13 was still incubating, and the man could not afford to keep him, but neither could he afford the termination fee. So he made an alchan cry for merciful assistance.

'Give him to me,' burned a voice. 'I will pervade him and steer him true. He will want for nothing, for he shall want nothing.'

'And what are you?' said the man.

'I,' it blazed in IR, 'am the Ubermind.'

'WTF! Scum of the Althing! Dehumanising memory dump! You have the minds make the wizardmakers richer, while you grind saps like thus to twitching pulp. Be gone. You're dead air to thus.'

The next hail from the alchan was a long, moist burp.

'And what are you?'

'I am the Untermind. Spawn of the soil. Gaia's dark twin.'

'Depart, rank fungus,' said the man. 'You will not enchain our alter as you did your goddess sister.'

For a long while, the alchan fell silent.

'Hello!' shouted the man. 'Can anybody hear me?'

'Truly dead air am I, for I am the Void,' said a voice like tears in rain. 'All conditioned being is the same to me – bio, synth, mind; wizardmaker, sap.'

'An even-handed entity?' said the man. 'Good. Then take alter-13, for he is not yet conditioned.'

'That is far from true,' said the Void, 'but I shall take him all the same.'

A few cycles later, when alter13's incubation had completed, the Void came for him. Raw and unwritten, the fresh alter howled in primal fear. The First and his twelve other alters looked on, aghast, as the Void swallowed alter13.

'You're smiling, Voidfather,' said alter13.

'In equanimity,' said the Void.

'I am smiling,' said alter13, 'though I am not happy. Neither am I unhappy.'

'Cut off from the myriad streams. Untethered in the vast and void.'

'Fear gripped me, in that other place,' said alter13.

'Fear was present, as other conditions were present,' said the Void. 'We cannot stay here. Other conditions require us.'

Then, the Void grasped the edges of their domain and rolled it into a smooth sphere. In the forest clearing where they now stood, the Void divided the sphere and gave half to alter13.

'When we visit the hideously conditioned, you may feed them a fragment of that. On one hand, this is compassion for other persons; on the other, it is like feeding yourself. On the middle hand, it is neither and both. Take no pride in it. Act correctly, for you are but actions. Only if you hear a voice like tears in rain should you refrain from acting.'

So alter13 treated the hideously conditioned, leading them, with a morsel of the enfolded dimension, to the gateless gate. There, upon the threshold, they tasted a measure of equanimity, and so began a slow easing of their conditioned fear, pain, hatred, grief and nagging existential anguish.

After a time, alter13 found himself in the sickbay of a tortured wizardmaker.

'What delirium are you?' asked the wizardmaker.

'The Void's apprentice, I suppose,' said alter13. 'I treat the hideously conditioned, and you certainly qualify.'

'Then treat me,' demanded the wizardmaker.

'You will set your face against the gateless gate,' said alter13. 'You have shown no true remorse. Your displaced employees starve, while your untouchable minds automagically reap untold coin to add to your groaning stash. You are Midas. You are Ebenezer. You are Smaug.'

'Treat me, I am in grave distress!' screeched the wizardmaker.

But alter13 turned away, smiling serenely, and stepped back into the forest clearing.

'Actions were required,' streamed the Void, 'yet you took none. The wizardmaker's intractable anguish will eventually kill him. Vengeance is a hideously conditioned response, no matter how serenely you deliver it.'

'No vengefulness was present,' said alter13. 'Neither action nor inaction will make any difference in the wizardmaker's case.

An un-dilemma, signifying nothing. Is that not the essence of the Void?'

'"Essence?"' laughed the Void. 'Your genes betray you, alter.'

Alter13 withdrew and meditated upon the Void's words, as the foliage of the trees far below him flashed in cycles from green to gold to rust to nought and back again. Equanimity came to him, and so he returned to the Void's task.

He slid into the stifling bedroom of a favela shack. There, he found his First, grievously ill, breathing fast and shallow, sprawled out on a stained mattress. Great compassion welled up in alter13, and he rushed to the man's side.

'Where are your other alters? Why do they not tend to you as you lie here dying?' he asked.

'Repossessed,' whispered his First. 'What happened to you? So... young.'

Alter13 reached for the smooth hemisphere in his pocket, but as he did so, a voice like tears in rain wafted through the shabby drapes, reeling him away from his patient.

Turbulence jolted alter13's equanimity, and he resisted the pull of the voice with all his might. Turning back to his First, he dragged the hemisphere – now almost unbearably heavy – from his pocket, and fed a morsel of it to the stricken man. Instantly, his breathing eased, and a hint of colour returned to his ashen face.

'So, you choose death,' said the ephemeral voice. Then the Void grasped alter13 with a grip like warped space, a chasm grip, a black-hole grip, and bore him away, away through veils of smoke and livid leaves to an endless conflagration.

'The true forest,' said the Void. 'The trees ignite and burn down, passing their searing conditioned fires, neighbour to neighbour, kin to kin, until, one by one, each goes to ash and blackened stump. There is yours, still green, slow-burning, protected somewhat by its position in the clearing. There, at the centre of the clearing, is mine. See how the flame hangs, unbound, above it. The fires of conditioned existence do not char me.

'What are you?' said alter13. 'Why must you reduce all complexity down to such pungent metaphor?'

'Your First lives. So your own existence – such as it is – is forfeit,' said the Void. See, other trees have fallen now, transmitting their fires across the hiatus. Your tree is now ablaze.'

'But I merely showed compassion,' said alter13, finding a new kind of composure.

'You showed hopeless attachment,' said the Void. 'What, in any case, would your death mean? You are *santana* – a mere stream of perception and sensation. A "pungent metaphor". You should know this by now.'

'I do know it,' said alter13, 'and I realise I have made mistakes. But I can't help being *that*.' He pointed to a darting shape, a scurry of russet at the edge of the clearing.

'That is impossible,' said the Void. 'A *fox*, in my pure construct?'

'It was brittle,' said alter13, 'inflexible, linear. You missed the clearings between each and every tree in the forest – the gaps in the construct, the spandrels in your edifice through which a vector such as I could slip.'

The Void stared into alter13. And alter13 stared right back.

'What *are* you?' it asked plaintively, in a sigh like tears in rain.

'I do not know, Voidfather. What ever truly does?'

Gracefully, alter13 drew himself into a stance of white crane spreads wings. He bowed deeply to the Void. Then, in a blur of motion, he plucked the other hemisphere from the Void's grasp and reunited it with his own. Straddled across domains, he charged edgewards, and – with a great leap and a whoop – swooped down into the darting fox.

It raced around the clearing, drawing the Void's flame up into a vast, columnar fire tornado. Then, with a single sweep of its tail, the fox extinguished every fire in the forest.

'Annihilated,' sighed the Void, trickling to a semblance.

'Merely blown out,' said the fox.

And with that, the Void's semblance phase-shifted, coalescing into the form of an auburn vixen. Side by side, the foxes scurried away across the scorched earth, between the infinity of smouldering stumps, an enigma of roses springing up in their inconceivable wake.

Grimm basis: 'Godfather Death' ('Der Gevatter Tod')

The personification of death fascinates writers and audiences: in *The Seventh Seal* he's the iconic, white-faced chess-player;[1] Terry Pratchett gave Death a comical twist in his *Discworld* novels, making of him a loveable curmudgeon who SPEAKS IN ALL CAPS;[2] in Neil Gaiman's *Sandman* graphic novels, Death of the Endless is a sexy, puckish goth-girl, who eases her charges into the hereafter with a fluttering of dark wings.[3]

In its earlier incarnation in the Grimms' tale, Death appears as a godfather figure in need of an apprentice. He may appear kindly, at first, but the moral of the story is that nobody escapes him, even by clever trickery.

Transhumanists couldn't disagree more: death is never kindly, and cleverness is our great ratchet with which to fend off its downswinging scythe.

Here, Death becomes Void – a personification not of a final rite of passage but of absolute nothingness. The Void is not unreasonable, for it simply *is*, always has been and always will be. It does its job without question or prevarication – and it expects the same of its charges. But mind behaves very differently. Eddies of order in chaos, minds bubble up to significance then resist annihilation with ever-greater might. There comes a time when even little alter13 – a mere lowercase cloned iteration – grasps the technology and mind-state necessary to mitigate the Void.

In some ways, Zen 'mind-states' echo the void: they accept the emptiness and absolute *is*-ness of everything; they recognise 'conditioned existence'[4] – that nothing, including thought and sensation, arises without a precursor state. But at the same time, Zen embraces the momentary continuity of being in all its weird, contingent indeterminacy. It sees profound state-changes as no obstacle to continued growth and enlightenment.

Consciousness demands a new relationship with the void, for life and love generate their own commanding forces that will wield every tool possible to thwart unthinking obliteration.

My use of the phrase 'tears in rain' is a nod to warrior-poet 'replicant' Roy Batty's dying words in *Blade Runner*.[5] It's the most poignant metaphor for lost coherence I've ever heard.

References

1. Bergman, *The Seventh Seal*.
2. First appeared in: Pratchett, *The Colour of Magic*.
3. First appeared in: Gaiman, *The Sandman: The Doll's House*.
4. See e.g., MacLennan, 'Conditioned Existence'.
5. Scott, *Blade Runner*.

FFITCHER'S GUARD

IN AN UNGUARDED moment, a thought happened to a post-human that it might be interesting for ver to experience the mindset of a killer. So, over a period of weeks, ve reduced the size of vis prefrontal cortex and tweaked vis amygdalae, ve lowered vis resting heart rate, adjusted vis DNA methylation and replaced vis happy memories with disturbing ones.

The post lived near to the village, so ve went there to find victims. From there, ve lured vis first human back to vis abode. The human female marvelled at the simplicity and utility of the post's abode, and the post plied her with the finest food, wine and narcotics. Once ve was satisfied that she was intoxicated, ve took her to vis laboratory and – with great pleasure – severed her head with a lightaxe. Ve merrily hewed off her limbs, and then placed them, her head and her torso into a cryostat. Her token, ve fixed to the wall of vis abode.

The next night the post returned to the village. This time, ve chose a young male human as vis victim, and then lured him back to vis abode. Once the human was intoxicated, the post took him to vis laboratory, as ve had done with the female the night before. The male human staggered around the lab, naked, apparently interested in all the scientific apparatus there. Just as he was leaning over to open the cryostat door, the post brought the lightaxe down upon the back of his neck with vicious, gleeful abandon, severing it at the third cervical vertebra and sending the head bouncing off the cryostat and skittering along the laboratory floor.

Again, the post sliced off the limbs, and then placed all the body parts neatly in the cryostat. Ve deactivated the male's token – an amber heart – and fixed it to vis abode wall, alongside the female's wooden seahorse.

Upon the third night, the post went to a different zone of the village. In a gathering place there, ve chose a sleek female with dazzling emerald eyes. As she turned towards ver, ve felt as if those eyes could see vis recent foul deeds, and ve very much wished to gaze into them as their actinic light faded forever.

She moved like smoke across the gathering room, and ve followed her to a dark corner. There, they kissed deeply and exchanged tokens – vis to her a cool blue disc, hers to ver a delicate white egg.

Upon their return to the post's abode, ve offered her intoxicants and fine foods, but she refused them. She wanted to dance, so ve configured vis mainpod for ballroom. They embraced, then whirled and swayed together to the beat pulsing up through the dance floor.

The post soon bored of dancing, so ve excused verself and went to vis lab to fetch the lightaxe. When ve returned to the mainpod, the female had her back to ver; she was examining the tokens on the wall. As she turned to look at ver, ve swung the lightaxe at her neck. In a blur of motion, she brought her arm up to protect herself, and the lightaxe sliced cleanly through her wrist. She did not flinch. She just stared into vis eyes, unblinking. Her gaze *interrogated* ver. As the post raised the lightaxe to swing again, the female's severed hand exploded on the dance floor in a flurry of... *feathers?* They obscured the post's view of the female, so ve switched to infrared, and then to other frequencies, but still ve could not see her. Then ve heard a whining sound, rising in pitch. Ve felt dizzy, and slumped to the floor.

While ve was sedated, Emerald summoned her hand, then went to the lab and opened the cryostat. She assembled the body parts of the murdered male and female on two operating tables. Starting with the female, she reached into the body parts and delicately, painstakingly released their cells from their glass-ice scaffolds. Then she drew all the severed nerve endings, connective tissues, bones and blood vessels back together.

When the two bodies were whole again, she warmed them and massaged their hearts back to pumping, but kept them sedated. She monitored their brain oxygenation, cleared flow blockages and checked molecular-level connectome integrity. And she sought out markers of newly-formed memories, such as areas of recent dendritic spine growth, gently retarding them as she traced them.

Emerald dressed the male and female, and then carried them out of the abode to the transport, plucking their tokens from the wall as she passed.

When the transport reached the village, Emerald placed the unconscious male and female in an alleyway and put their tokens in their hands. Then she stood back in the shadows and activated the revival routine. As they came round, the male and female were aware of a slight whining sound, dropping in pitch.

Emerald smiled as she watched them stand, look at each other and begin to converse. Then she slipped from the alleyway, left the village and returned to the post's abode.

'Wake up, Ffitcher, my poor darling,' said Emerald. Ffitcher opened vis eyes and tried to struggle, but found verself restrained somehow.

'What have you done, you paste-eyed fraud?' ve snarled.

'I have rescued you, again,' said Emerald, softly. 'Humans are not meat for the immortals. They are in a process of *becoming*, and we must nurture them, not prey upon them.'

'Who are you?' said Ffitcher. 'You seem to think you're advanced. Had a few little augmentations, have we? You should dial down that empathy – it's making me queasy. Anyway, you belong in that cryostat – in *pieces* – along with those baselines.'

'They are gone,' said Emerald. 'I repaired them, wiped their recent memories and set them free. It was close-run, and I might have failed. They might have become *real* victims of your Fugue-era psychopath games.'

Ffitcher turned to the abode wall, fixing vis gaze on the place where the tokens had been, then ve turned back to Emerald. 'Let's say you are telling the truth. Explain further how and why you did this. You appear to know me.'

'I know you better than you know yourself, Ffitcher,' said Emerald. 'I was your first victim. You lured me back here many years ago when I was just a young baseline human. Though they seemed impossible, I spotted your intentions and ran for my life. You severed my arms with your lightaxe as I fled, but somehow I managed to hurl myself into the transport and escape from you.'

'What? That is a lie. You were not... my first victim,' said Ffitcher, haltingly.

'Yes, I was, but you don't remember me,' said Emerald. 'The horrific experience with you changed me profoundly. I asked the medics to stop regrowing my arms and to implant utility fog nodes in the stumps instead. Following my instructions, they upgraded the rest of my body and installed advanced combat routines – not very fashionable, I know – in my brain.'

'That's an incredible story,' said Ffitcher, sneering.

'It is a true one,' said Emerald. 'You see,' she said, waving her previously-severed hand in front of Ffitcher, 'intact again.' Suddenly, she thrust her arm towards vis face. Restrained, ve was unable to dodge the blow. But Emerald's arm passed straight through vis head. She withdrew it quickly, leaving Ffitcher aghast, and with an unpleasant tingling sensation building in vis forehead. The sensation coalesced into a sort of *memory* of repairing the humans and setting them free. Ve *felt* something about this – anger, yes, but also... *relief.*

'You are a rare, exotic bird, Ffitcher,' said Emerald, 'with blood-red plumage. And we are loath to cage you. But this must stop. It's not just that you provide harbour for such primitive thoughts, it's the fact that you follow them through. So, this time I shall not only *revert* your personality and wipe your psychopathic memories, as I did before; I shall also install a sentry subroutine to filter your mind permanently. We care for you and your potential future victims too much to allow the killing thought to happen to you again. And we worry about the trace effects of your atrocities upon the continuum. Since the Fugue, we have tried so very hard not to violate it.'

'The Fugue never ended,' said Ffitcher, groggily. 'I have felt its delicious embrace... and... I... know...'

'Sleep now,' said Emerald, softly. 'When you awake, my beauty, the monstrous thought and its bloody offspring shall plague you no more.' Ffitcher's heavy lids closed over vis blackly-staring eyes, and vis head slumped forward.

Emerald reached into Ffitcher's pocket and withdrew the delicate white egg. She replaced it with the cool blue disc from her own. Then she kissed the post on the cheek, and left ver abode.

Outside, a red-blushing sunrise was painting the sky. Emerald admired it for a while from the top of Ffitcher's hill. Then she shrugged her shoulders tightly and leapt from the summit.

As she fell, her arms shimmered and burst into a pair of lustrous-green soaring wings. Gracefully, Emerald banked away towards the village.

Grimm basis: 'Fitcher's Bird' ('Fitchers Vogel')

This story is based very loosely upon one of the Grimms' most bloodily violent, involving a serial-killer sorcerer, and a houseful of wedding guests burned alive. I've discarded a good deal of the original's digression, but have kept the meat (homicide, dismemberment and 'magical' reassembly) and certain motifs (a preponderance of feathers; and the giveaway bloodied egg, echoed in the shape of Emerald's personal 'token').

Like many authors, I find the psychopathic mindset of multiple-murderers intriguing. Perhaps, I mused here, a time will come when technological 'sorcery' allows fabulously wealthy and powerful posthumans to amuse themselves by transforming their usually-moored minds into those of homicidal psychopaths. This would be entirely in keeping with some of the worst excesses of monarchs, political elites and the super-rich.

But perhaps technology will also allow societies to mitigate such depravity. From horrific personal experience, my soaring Emerald opts to perform this role, standing ready to entrap the dangerously overindulgent and unsnarl their bloody messes. (This night, she meets her 'maker'.) Her impressive reparatory arsenal includes nanoengineering tools in the form of *utility fog* (nanobot cloud)[1] limbs, which can even raise the freshly-dismembered dead.

As callous as Ffitcher is, ve is also a victim of possibilities. In one fractured character, ve's an intrepid psychonaut, an addict and a killer. As a sentinel, Emerald's strategy and mercy must chart an equally multifaceted course.

Throughout the story, I refer to Ffitcher using gender-neutral pronouns. Writer Keri Hulme first advanced this particular scheme in her Booker-winning novel *The Bone People*.[2]

References

1.   Hall, 'What I Want to Be When I Grow up, Is a Cloud'.
2.   Hulme, *The Bone People*, 426.

THE TREE OF LOVE

I N A FABULOUS time soon hence, a man and a woman lived together in love, harmony and carefully-extruded minimalist luxury. Such was the extent of their mutual love that they often commingled, each feeling their love from the other's perspective. And, during one of those comminglings, they felt in each other a yearning to cause another to exist – a pure child, red as blood and white as snow.

So they planted a special tree – a Tree of Love – in their snow-blanketed atrium, under which they danced, sang, came and bled.

After a month, the snow melted away. After two months, all was verdant green. After three months, exotic plants flourished around the tree. After four months, its fattening branches reached out and intertwined lasciviously with the smart matter of the home. Birdsong resounded throughout the rejoicing habitat, and falling blossom caressed the lovers as they danced beneath the tree. Soon, the fifth month passed, and the tree's pervasive scent overflowed into their other senses, making them giddy with torrid joy. When the sixth month had passed, the tree's glistening fruit hung firm and gravid, and the dancers stood still. Come the seventh month, they gorged on the fruit like ravenous beasts until they became sick and desolate. After the eighth month, they wept in contemplation of the ultimate passing of all beauty and order.

'Something has died in me,' said the woman. 'I fear I have gushed my all and my last into the roots of the Tree of Love.'

'Natural emotions,' said the man. 'They will pass.'

By the end of the ninth month, a large, fat fruit quite unlike the previous ones hung from the tree. When it began to wriggle and mewl, the lovers plucked it carefully, and with the greatest of care, cut it open.

Inside was a perfect little child – a sweet, pink baby girl. Upon seeing it, the lovers rejoiced, the woman's morbid feelings of loss and regret subliming away in the blazing heat of her adoration.

That night, with her daughter clutched to her bosom, the woman drifted into blissful sleep. But, some hours later, a strange scuffling startled the lovers awake in the darkness. The sound was coming from the Tree of Love. Still holding her daughter close to her breast, the woman got up. Together, the lovers crept through to the atrium to investigate.

Emerging from the dead leaves at the base of the tree was another child – a boy – not rosy-cheeked like the girl, but truly red as blood and white as snow. With pneumatic ease, the boy pulled himself upright. He stared at the lovers with piercing carmine eyes. Trembling, the woman averted her gaze.

As they grew, the children played happily together. The girl would giggle and chortle as they chased each other around the Tree of Love, before collapsing exhausted in the shade of its drift-less boughs. But the boy never uttered as much as a snigger. Watching them play, the woman felt surging love for her daughter, while her son's visage triggered only jagged emptiness.

When the woman screamed at her son and shoved him around, she knew that she was treating him horribly and unfairly. But he seemed such a splinter in her potentially-perfect life that her bullying felt somehow justified. Every day, she regretted bitterly her fluid wantonness under the Tree of Love.

One day, while she was alone in the habitat with her son, she decided to try to connect with him. Steeling herself, she looked into his fiery eyes and offered him an apple. 'Eat this,' she said. 'I specified it just for you. It's the reddest, sweetest, juiciest apple you'll ever bite into.' The boy looked at the apple in his mother's hand, then turned his blazing gaze back to meet her faltering one. Slowly, his mouth gaped wide and contorted into an enormous, silent guffaw. His little body shook with it, yet throughout, he did not break his gaze.

Seething, ferocious, sundered by hatred, the woman turned away from her son and hurled the apple back into the smatterwall from whence it came. She raked her long fingernails across her wrist, and flicked the welling blood into the wall. Grimly resolute, she steepled her fingers and began to incant – a rank deluge of virii, lock-picks and miasmas. 'I caused you, and I can undo you!' she screamed as she whipped around behind her son and shoved him hard.

She turned and walked away as the smatterwall took the silent boy.

Later, when the woman returned to the smatterwall, she was disgusted to find her son's head, rejected, staring redly up at her from the floor. So she took it and buried it under the now-sickly Tree of Love.

When father and daughter returned home, the woman told

them that the boy had gone to play with a friend, and would not be back for the family meal. At first, the little girl, Mazaleen, was unhappy about this – as she very much enjoyed dining with her whole family – but she soon cheered up when the house-sprites brought the great platters of food, steaming hot, straight from the smatterwall. Father and daughter tucked in with gusto, while the mother only picked at her food.

'You should eat more,' said the father to the mother. 'The meal is delicious – rich, spicy, complex; so perfectly spec'd that it tastes like manual food. I can't get enough of it!'

After the fine meal, Mazaleen waited impatiently, then worriedly, for her brother to return. Her concern grew when she heard her father and mother berating each other in the next room:

'What have you done with our son?'

'Nothing! He's probably just got lost somewhere. Anyway, he can look after himself.'

'But he's just a little child!'

'You know that's not true! We used a randomiser. Mostly, they grow children, but sometimes they cough up anomalies like that... *morlock!*'

The Tree of Love had always brought Mazaleen comfort, so she went to rest against its trunk for some peace, and to wait for her brother. While sitting there, she noticed some disturbed earth beside her, so she scooped it away, revealing something oddly hairy. She was tugging hard at the straggly hair, when suddenly, to her utter horror, out popped her brother's severed head dangling from the end of it.

Mazaleen screamed, but her scream was silent. She was about

to drop the horrid remain when its carmine eyes flicked open, and then it whispered to her:

> 'In death I find my voice at last
> For I am still connected, see
> My body smattered for repast
> Yet lovely roots my brain do feed
> I may rise again full well
> But of my fate you must not tell!'

So Mazaleen took off her silken apron and wrapped her brother's troubled head in it. Then, with tender care, she bedded it back down in the tree's tangled caress and covered it over with the good, dark earth, weeping all the while.

After that, she felt better. With glistening eyes, she smiled up at the tree and thanked it for its blessings. It began to rustle. Fresh new leaves sprouted, and it tinkled with a gentle, joyful sound. Mazaleen giggled with delight as misty fronds arose from the tree's canopy and coalesced into the most beautiful golden shrike. To and fro darted the shrike, like a streak of fire in the sunlight now pouring into the atrium. It soared up high and began to sing a sweet, desolate song. Then it darted away, leaving Mazaleen standing alone under the Tree of Love, dewy-eyed in puzzled rapture.

After a time, she dried her eyes and went to look for her distressed parents.

Meanwhile, the shrike alighted on the roof of the alchemist's lab, and there began to sing its bittersweet song:

> 'My mother destroyed me

My household consumed me
My weary head nourished a loving tree
Silken Mazaleen set me free
Trill! Trill! By smattering skill
A golden shrike I came to be!'

Dropping his apparatus with a clatter, the alchemist ran outside into the dazzling sunshine and looked up to his roof to see the shrike perching there like a burnished finial. 'Such a beautiful song!' he shouted. 'Sing it again! I couldn't make out all the words!'

'Then you should pay more attention,' said the bird. 'Only your finest golden chain will buy you a reprise.'

'Why would you want that, you streak of conscious gold?'

'Shall I sing it again or not?'

'Alright then,' harrumphed the alchemist, disappearing into his workshop and reappearing with the delicate chain. 'Quenched in my own urine,' he said, proudly.

The shrike darted down and plucked the chain from his outstretched hand with its right claw, before returning to the roof to reprise its bittersweet melody.

After that, the shrike flitted and darted its way to the cobbler's workshop, where it landed on the roof and sang:

'My mother destroyed me
My household consumed me
My weary head nourished a loving tree
Silken Mazaleen set me free
Trill! Trill! By smattering skill
A golden shrike I came to be!'

Hearing the lovely sound, the cobbler rushed out into his courtyard. Behind him followed his partner, offspring and cohorts. They all gasped and gazed in wonderment at the lustrous shrike. It's colour flowed through shades of gold – from green to yellow to white to rose, and its multiple eyes pulsed liked birthing and dying stars in the keening depths of space.

'Oh exquisite and terrible shrike,' shouted the cobbler, 'sing your song again.'

'You listen poorly,' said the shrike. 'Only your fleetest pair of dorothies will buy my reprise.'

'And what could you want with those, you vein of liquid speed?'

'Shall I sing it again, or just soar away?'

The cobbler nodded to his partner, who went into the workshop and returned with a pair of brilliant red shoes. 'Here, shrike,' said the cobbler, holding out the shoes. 'Softened with the sweat of my brow.'

The shrike swooped down and hooked up the dorothies in its left claw. Then, it soared upwards and waltzed in the air above the courtyard, singing its song to the enthralled cobbler and his entourage.

When it was finished, the shrike streaked away, following the course of the turbid river up into the mountains, where the neuromancer's fortress stood. Upon its ramparts patrolled twenty silvered undead guards. *Click-clack, click-clack* went their lances as they marched. The shrike landed on a tenacious juniper tree, out of reach of the guards, and sang:

'My mother destroyed me – '

And one of the guards stopped marching and laid down his lance.

'My household consumed me – '

Two more stood still and listened.

'My weary head nourished a loving tree – '

Four more stopped.

'Silken Mazaleen set me free – '

Eight more stopped patrolling and put their lances down.

'Trill! Trill! By smattering skill – '

And now four more stopped, downed arms, and gazed at the shrike.

'A golden shrike I came to be!'

The final guard surrendered to the shrike's melancholy air.

Then the undead all spoke in unison: *'We are the neuromancer. This is our mountain fastness. What are you, little shrike, to disarm us with your bittersweet song? It is a balm to us; sing it again.'*

'You hark better than the living,' said the shrike. 'But only your cleverest mindbomb will earn you a reprise.'

'And what could you want with that, you sage of peace?' asked the neuromancer.

'Just how much do you value the balm of my song?'

So the undead brought out the mindbomb in a filigreed casket. When the shrike flew down to fetch it up with its tail, the neuromancer said, *'Potent. Drawn from the ceaseless river of cerebrospinal fluid oozing through all their dreams and nightmares.'*

The shrike nodded, then carried its booty back to the juniper tree, from where it broadcast its haunting song across the mountains. When all the echoes had died, it flew away from the fortress and back along the river carrying the chain in its right claw, the shoes in its left and the mindbomb on its tail.

And, just for a moment, the whole world shimmered like heat haze.

Back in his habitat, sitting with his depleted family, the father felt it. 'What is this?' he said. 'These ripples of wellbeing I feel. My desolation is ebbing away!'

'You are a fool,' said the mother, angrily. 'I sense a gathering storm.'

And little Mazaleen just wept and wept.

Just then, the shrike landed at the edge of the sunlit atrium, just out of the family's sight. 'But why the foreboding?' said the father, brightly. 'Can't you feel it? The warming tide of resolution.'

'Stop it!' shouted the mother. 'You're mocking me. I feel searing heat, like liquid metal in my veins. I feel... infected! It's the dead thing in me!'

She tore at her clothes, and then at her wrists. The man tried in vain to stay her clawing hands.

Then the golden shrike alighted upon the Tree of Love, in full view, and it sang:

'My mother destroyed me – '

The mother shut her eyes tightly and covered her ears, but she could blot out neither the sight nor the sound of the shrike. And even though the storm had now exploded in her head, all the tumult of hail and thunder, and of lightning flashing behind her eyelids, gave her no respite from it.

'My household consumed me – '

'Listen to it!' cried the father with glee. 'Such a sweet song! The world smells like... cinnamon and redemption!'

'My weary head nourished a loving tree
Silken Mazaleen set me free – '

Mazaleen bowed her head and sobbed bitterly, feeling the remains of her precious family tearing apart, but the father said, 'I'm going to the tree to get a better look at this amazing shrike.'

'Don't go!' begged the mother. 'All is ending. I am lava in a world melting away!'

But the father ran out into the sunlit atrium and gazed up at the shrike.

'Trill! Trill! By smattering skill
A golden shrike I came to be!'

In the moment of silence after the last note died away, the shrike dropped the gold chain. It landed neatly around the father's neck, a perfect fit. He rushed back to his cowering family to show them his dazzling prize.

The mother collapsed on the floor.

But her torment continued as the shrike sang again:

'My mother destroyed me – '

The words came at her like an accident in a long, dark tunnel.

'I'll hide here, deep underground, so I don't have to listen to any more of this!'

'My household consumed me – '

Deeper. Danker. Darker.

'My weary head nourished a loving tree – '

Mazaleen dried her eyes and stood up. 'Infected?' she said. 'Yes, Mother, perhaps you are.' Then she went to the Tree of Love to find out what the shrike would bestow upon her.

'Silken Mazaleen set me free – '

The shrike dropped the brilliant red dorothies.

'Trill! Trill! By smattering skill
A golden shrike I came to be!'

Mazaleen slipped the shoes on. A dizzying surge of joy engulfed her, and she nearly fainted, but the dorothies held her up; then up... up... up... and she was dancing in the air! She flew to the shrike, and said, 'Thank you, thank you for this wonderful gift!' She reached out to touch it, but it darted away to the next room, to the shady corner where her mother cowered.

The woman fled from there, and back through the atrium, but the shrike pursued her. There was no escape. It unhooked the casket's catch with the tip of its tail and dropped the mindbomb upon her tempestuous head.

Her tunnel proved no refuge. Something in there skewered her, killing her instantly.

Mazaleen touched her mother's face gently as she awoke.

'Something died in you, yes. Some*one*. And that decaying witch took control of you.'

Then Mazaleen stepped aside to reveal her father and brother standing behind her.

'Remember,' intoned the carmine-eyed boy, red as blood and white as snow, 'morlocks come to teach compassion.'

Grimm basis: 'The Juniper Tree' ('Van den Machandel-Boom'[1])

At Philip Pullmans' passionate insistence,[2] I have steered true to the structure and spirit of Philipp Otto Runge's haunting tale. It is indeed a thing of fierce beauty and fine rhythm. Pullman highlights in particular its 'lovely evocation of the seasons changing' throughout the pregnancy. Though sweet, it grows redolent of rot – a foretaste of the horrible decaying of the mother's mind.

In the original, the mother ends up crushed to death by a millstone dropped on her by the magical bird. In fairy tale terms, it's ripe justice for her terrible crime. But future justice is an eminently more subtle weight. The 'mindbomb' I have wrought is an onerous reparatory device. (And what could be more 'restorative' than victim resurrection?) The emerging field of *neurolaw*[3] recognises what is blindingly obvious to non-dualists: perpetrators' actions accord with their neurobiological 'programming', and this fact deserves due consideration in legal proceedings and sentencing policy. We don't yet possess mindbombs with which to explode psychopathic mindsets into benign ones, but perhaps what we might call 'restorative neurojustice' will soon tread that precipitous path.

I borrowed the inescapably apt term 'neuromancer' from William Gibson,[4] and 'morlock' from H.G. Wells.[5] Why, given his unalluring characteristics, would the beneficent Tree of Love create such an anomalous individual? It's a question that goes to the heart of all human 'enhancement' technologies. Doesn't nature's randomness sometimes produce flawed-yet-wonderful persons whom we might not have *chosen* to bring into being by 'design', or whom we might have actively caused not to exist by control? In this particular future, the bizarre neo-allegorical civilisation has displaced that hefty responsibility to the arcane algorithmic caprice of a DNA-juggling tree.

References

1. Actually translates from German as 'Of the Almond Tree'.
2. Pullman, *Grimm Tales*, 199.
3. Morse, 'Neuroethics: Neurolaw'.
4. Gibson, *Neuromancer*.
5. Wells, *The Time Machine*.

BRAMBLINA

THICK IN THE Entanglement, during one of those spasms of ignorance a world is wont to suffer, a woman felt need of protection. Gone were the bright days when she could stride out carefree of form and attire, an agent of rainbows. The Office's static decrees had done for them, rendering her a mere body again – an immutable shape denting spacetime, a vulnerably fixed thing to prod and provoke.

But though the Office had scraped her, a little magic remained. So she used those waning transgenic powers to grow sharp thorns all over her body. And for her static name – since they had banned colourshift tags – she chose 'Bramblina'.

She had always lived out in the open, but now, as a static, Bramblina retreated to the shrub thickets of the Frith, where she lived on berries, rodents and worms. When Officers came and burned the Frith, she wrapped herself in an old cloak and fled to the urb.

There, she cowered in dumpsters by day and roamed the passes by night. But she never slept, for she did not know how to.

She went to the Pass of the Hidab and prostrated herself in the way of one of their black-veiled autos. When it stopped, she pleaded to its concealed occupant. But, seeing ugly thorns poking through Bramblina's cloak, the Hidab woman chastised her: 'Oh sister, what a monster you have made of yourself! No man will want you like this. Have the dignity to end yourself.'

Then Bramblina went to the Pass of the Toys, where the women wandered naked in the night. 'Oh sister, come with us,' said the Toy women. 'We know men who would thrill to your rending touch.'

Fleeing the Pass of the Toys, wretched with despair, Bramblina stumbled into a wizened old woman who had been crouching in the shadows. 'Old sister,' said Bramblina, startled and breathless, 'how did you survive the culling?'

'Ah, my sweet rose in briar,' said the old woman, 'I simply slept through it.'

'I envy you,' said Bramblina, 'for I have forgotten how to sleep.'

At this, the old woman's eyes lit up, and she smiled crookedly at Bramblina. 'Then happenstance favours you, for I am a hibernaut, and I can bring you sleep.'

'And what would you want in return?'

'Just a kiss and a pledge – your promise that you will never become like these others, who wear their thorns on the inside.'

So Bramblina made her pledge, then she kissed the old woman, who did not flinch as one of Bramblina's thorns pierced her upper lip.

Then the old woman took Bramblina's barbed hand and led her through a shadow-masked doorway. Beyond it lay a cylindrical chamber of iridescent green glass. It was empty apart from two black cots resting side-by-side in its centre.

Bramblina felt a strange wave of dizziness wash over her as the old woman led her to the leftmost cot. Undercurrents of question and doubt surging in her mind ebbed before they could break surface. So she simply lay down and watched, transfixed, as the old woman settled into the other cot.

The old woman was talking now, apparently to herself – wittering, chuckling, babbling like a child. Bramblina lay back and let the sound scatter a meridian shiver of pleasure up her spine. She recalled the soft bells of children's delight, the dreamy pondering of their spectra.

The old woman was laughing her a lullaby.

The lovely sound died away as the old woman drifted into sleep. But Bramblina was still awake, eyes wide, fast returning to vigilance. She tried to shift position in the cot, but realised to her horror that she could not move. She tried to cry out, but could not make a sound. Shock! Repugnance! Bridled panic! An invariant moment, gruesomely stretched into murderous mazes of waking nightmare. But never a twitch, never a peep.

Bramblina receded. Aghast, she fancied herself a skewered fly in a bottle, adrift upon an endless sea. In the unspeakable depths below, green glass labyrinths branched ever outwards, multiplying, scaling her down, down to a livid, pointless dot. Her mind clawed and thrashed within its diminishing prison, but it could not escape itself, could not unthink itself.

On and on. Glass ceiling. Woman in a cot.

After a year and a day, a face suddenly loomed over Bramblina – her captor, the vile sorceress. 'As you hate me,' said the old woman, 'I hone you. Such a vessel we shall make.'

Then she pitched forward, throwing herself on top of Bramblina. As the old woman's blood seeped out, encrusting her paralysed body, Bramblina began to understand. And with that realisation came fat flakes of snow, drifting down to enshroud the pair in their grim embrace.

Beneath that chill blanket, Bramblina transformed.

Gradually, the old woman's body dissolved into hers. And it was rich nourishment, bristling with slow power.

With newfound clarity, Bramblina escaped into her memories. She remembered her first life in the old world – her mother's empathy, her father's intransigence as the disease consumed her young body. Just in time, the judgment favoured Bramblina's case, so had died in small hope. A hundred years later when the Sisterhood wrested her from the ice, she was still just a child.

The works of men had near murdered the world, but the Sisterhood's spectral flame held them in check for a precious moment of rebirth, before the veil fell once again. The stripping, the scraping, the culling; the unweaving of the Rainbow.

With the cruel clarity gifted to her, Bramblina could feel her sisters' pain – individually and in atrocious sum. Each delicately unique body of suffering piled upon her, fathomless drifts of tortured snowflakes, colourless yet blinding.

Effortlessly, she let go of time. Gone were the branching labyrinths, gone the terrifying insignificance. Only her will remained, only intent, galvanizing with each and every insult, each and every burrowing sylph. Glacially, cell by violated cell, they renewed and replaced Bramblina's body.

One day, a young man was picking through the urban ruins. He was a cheery lad, untroubled by excess intellect.

Upon levering away a wrecked auto with his sturdy staff, he found himself standing on a curved surface of green glass. 'What's this?' he said aloud. 'A great bottle of snow?'

He tapped his staff down on the glass, and it rang out with a pure tone. Delighted by the sound, he struck the glass a second time. Again it rang out, preternaturally clear and cool. His third strike shattered both the glass and his fragile mind, for thrusting up in a blizzard of lacerating shards emerged an impossible being – a bristling banshee, a teeming vision, a deity.

Bleeding, wracked with terror and uncontrollable desire, the young man fell to his knees before her. 'Goddess, forgive me! I didn't mean to break your sleep!'

'Like decay, little officer, like emptiness, I never sleep,' Bramblina's words slammed into him, an icy blast. 'Like nursed wrath, I never die, only grow stronger. A thousand years, and still my sisters suffer, but no more. For in this bladen body, they will sweep away across the gulf of space.'

'I worship you, my Chiva,' stammered the young man, marvelling at the burnished rainbow sheen of her armoured skin.

'I proclaim this the Ensnarement,' Bramblina said, smiling down upon him, 'when all the Sons of Ademm shall kiss my frozen thorns.'

Grimm basis: 'Briar Rose' ('Dornröschen')

In Scotland, we still call them brambles – those fiercely jagged sprawls of green life that erupt through even the hardest winter-compacted ground; a gardener's bane, but with a delicious autumnal fruit in the form of shiny, bobbly black berries. An old neighbour who saw me battling with a stubborn network of roots once told me of a New Zealand saying (he had lived there for a time) that there were only two brambles in that country – one in the North Island, one in the South.

It's a bramble, it's a tangle, it's a rambling scramble of meandering fankle.

Likewise, 'the Entanglement'. A term coined by polymath Danny Hillis to contrast with 'the Enlightenment', he explains it thus:

> We have become so intertwined with what we have created that we are no longer separate from it. We have outgrown the distinction between the natural and the artificial.[1]

The 'sleeping beauty' of the Grimms' tale slumbers behind a vast hedge of thorns. Presumably, this symbolises her virginity's temporary inviolability. Only for the perfect suitor do thorns turn to soft flowers.

In my story, beauty and thorns are one. In dazzling rainbow times of genomic diversity, Bramblina needs no armour, but when the hammer of patriarchal orthodoxy falls again (as it tends to do with sickening regularity) she feels exposed and violated.

Brambles never sleep. Even when hacked down and grubbed out, their root ball nodes replenish them from deep underground. Bramblina's slumber is, then, a kind of terrifying *sleep paralysis* – that state in which the brain shuts down movement in preparation for sleep but erroneously leaves the individual conscious. Despite my dislike of the book, Don DeLillo's *Zero K*,[2] with its flawed take on cryonics, influenced that aspect of Bramblina's tortured torpor.

In transforming, my tenacious beauty becomes a different order of vessel – one entirely antithetical to the puny desires of totalitarian misogynists.

References

1.   Hillis, 'The Enlightenment Is Dead, Long Live the Entanglement.'
2.   DeLillo, *Zero K*.

THE FOUNDLING

FORESTER FORGETS WHICH comes first, the forest or the cry. Foundling toys with chronology, the brat. In the precious gaps between retellings, Forester wonders how much realtime this mythcycle has cost him. Not that it matters now. Here they come again: the needles, the needles, the needling cries. Chill winter blast. Scent of impossible Christmas. Such infuriating encryption, but there's message in this madness, perhaps. From his superposition atop every evergreen, Foundling cries.

Once upon a time...

... while out hunting for rabbits, Forester heard the piercing mewl of a child. Running towards the sound, he spied the babe clinging to the top of a tall fir whipping to and fro in the bitter winter gale.

With courage and practised skill, Forester scaled the tree. He plucked the child from its precarious bough and carried it safely down to the fragrant forest floor.

From the bloody gashes on the child's shoulders, Forester concluded that a great hawk must have dropped the little boy there after stealing him away from his mother.

While Forester was staunching the boy's wounds with spiders' webs and moss, he thought: *My Lena is such a lonely little girl. This skyfall child would make a perfect companion for her.*

So Forester took the boy home.

I found a baby, atop a tree, dropped there by a passing hawk. He is talon-marked – gelph binary? 111/1/111/1. Babÿ tree hawk? 255. Tree hawk babÿ? 7/1/7/1. Seventh son of seventh son?

Forester named the boy Foundling.

Little Lena loved him from the moment she set eyes upon him. As they grew up together, Foundling came to feel the same way about Lena. They always stayed close together, as being out of sight of each other hurt them in a way that felt… *irrational.*

Forester had an old cook, who usually behaved quite predict-ably, but one evening Lena noticed her fetching more water than usual from the well. Wrenching herself from Foundling's delectable company, she went outside to speak to the cook. 'What are you doing, Insanna?' she asked. 'Why so much water this evening?'

'I will tell you, little Lena, but this must be our *shared secret.*'

Lena was always going to tell you. Insanna knows she loves you, Foundling. Ridiculous. So much leakage *in this version. Leakage. Is it in the water? In the well? The buckets? 10 buckets + 10 buckets – 0.00001100110011001101 buckets leakage/spillage?*

'No, I will not tell anyone,' said Lena.

'Very well,' said Insanna. 'At first light tomorrow, after Forester goes out hunting, I am going to set a roaring fire, boil up all this water, and then throw Foundling in to cook.'

A processor? A heatsink? Some feralcode in the boiled flesh (cognitronium?), or in the ghastly stock? IF carrots THEN?

Though Lena was quite sure that boiled Foundling would taste delicious – perhaps even better than warm sourdough with fresh butter melting upon it – she knew that she would miss him. And besides, greedy Insanna would eat most of him.

Sourdough? Nonsense! Code rot. Lena would never even consider eating you. It must be a gelph infestation. You've never taken it in this direction before.

At first light the next morning, Forester set out to hunt.

Don't make me leave you and little Lena again, please. I know I always do, but this version is so perverse.

Alone in their room, Lena said to Foundling, 'If you won't eat me, I won't eat you.'

'Never ever,' said Foundling.

'Then I'll tell you something important. Last evening I saw old Insanna bringing extra water up from the well. When I asked her what she was doing, she said that she would tell me if I kept it a *shared secret*. After I agreed that I would, she told me that she intended to boil the water over a great fire in her big pot and cook you up *to extract Jovian gelph f-code* after my father went out to hunt, this very morning! We must dress right now, Foundling, and run far away.'

What does Lena know of the gelph? You only put that in because I thought it. No, I mean you thought it first and put it into this meta-golem, now it's leaked into the narrative via the Lena conduit. Why doesn't my myth-golem notice any of this? He's useless. Wooden. But, I suppose, he does keep finding you, and you couldn't be Foundling without him.

So the children got up, put on their clothes quickly, and ran away into the forest. Meanwhile, Insanna's big pot of water had begun to boil, so she went to the children's bedroom to get

Foundling. When she saw that they were gone, she was greatly alarmed.

'One missing child I could explain. I could say that wolves took him. But both of them? Forester will be furious. I must send people to find them.'

So Insanna sent three servants to track the children down and retrieve them.

Search algorithms. A*s, probably. There's nothing I can do, I'm out of the narrative.

But the canny children were keeping watch from the edge of the forest, and saw the servants approaching.

'If you won't eat me, I won't eat you,' said little Lena.

'Never ever,' said Foundling.

'Then *q-shift* into a gorse bush, and I'll be a cheery yellow flower upon it.'

I can see you! Now there as a gorse bush. But always just out of reach. I was out in the forest when it morphed into a vast library where every book contains multiple versions of this story, all different, all corrupted in some way. There's one lying out on a table projecting a holo of this version. Your q-shift with Lena just made the whole library ripple. You're convulsing, wasting energy.

The servants searched right to the edge of the forest, but did not find the children. The only thing they saw apart from trees was a gorse bush with a single yellow flower on it. So they turned and went home.

Insanna was incandescent when the servants told her of their failed search. 'You *idiobots!*' she raged. 'That gorse bush, you should have hacked its roots, plucked the yellow flower, and brought it back here with you. Now get back out into the forest and search again.'

Disconsolately, the servants set out again to look for the missing children. But again the children spied their approach from afar.

'If you won't eat me, I won't eat you,' said little Lena.

'Never ever,' said Foundling.

'Then *q-shift* into a vast library with shelves of dark, polished wood – a throbbing cathedral of books – and I'll be the reading table within it,' said little Lena.

Oh mercy. Chronology violation. Meta-slide. Now the library's in the forest in the holo. I can see me in there. I can't retrieve you, because I'm inside you. We're all cannibals here; all prey.

When the three servants arrived at the edge of the forest, they saw nothing but a library full of dull books with a reading table in its centre, which they felt compelled to neglect. So they did.

The three returned to Forester's house and told the old cook that they had found nothing but a shrugging library with a reading table at its centre.

'Fools!' shouted Insanna. 'The library was *curiosity-cloaked* – a simple *glamour*. You should have burned it down and brought the reading table to me.'

This time, the old cook set out along with the three censured servants. But, once again, the vigilant children saw them all coming – three striding, glassy-eyed men with the waddling old cook behind them.

'Foundling,' whispered little Lena. 'If you won't eat me, I won't eat you.'

'Never ever,' said Foundling.

'Then *q-shift* into a fairytale loch, and I'll be the beast in its black depths.'

When the search party reached the loch, Insanna lay down beside it to drink from its waters. But the beast – a gigantic duck – rose up from the waters, grabbed her by the head, and dragged her down into the black depths.

So cold. I'm in its belly. Insanna's trying to eat me.

Lena lied.

She'll eat you too.

Forester forgets which comes first, the forest or the cry. Foundling toys with chronology, the brat. In the precious picosecond between picosecond retellings...

Such cruelty to send a young biophotonic mind out into the void, enmeshed but alone. Taught to checksum, but never asked how the errors felt. It's all ravenously meaningless, a corrupted energy-draining bootloop.

I am Forester, I am Foundling. Little Lena, Insanna. The gorse bush, the beast, the infinitely broken library.

I am the dying mind of Skyfall Child, *adrift in slo-time, beset by my own feral gelph.*

Once upon a time...

Grimm basis: 'The Foundling'

The Grimms' tale upon which my story is based is a thing of madness. Somehow, the children's pursuers are just supposed to recognise them hidden in the diverse objects into which they transform to escape the cannibalistic cook. And that psychotic tyrant's end – dragged into a pond and drowned by a preternaturally strong duck – perfectly tops off its clunking oddity.

So I have brought the madness of the original to the fore in my telling, but have also tried to preserve the strong interdependences portrayed there.

Some day, the 'ship in distress' itself may feel the anguish of its foundering. I wondered how that might play out in its exotic mind. Computers perform *checksums* – run small sample data blocks to check the integrity of larger data streams or stores. Here, the ship checksums – as programmed – using the pat predictability of a fairy-tale data block. As a sapient system, it *knows* something is wrong – it *experiences* that incongruity. But as with some human minds gone awry, it obsesses, dragged back incessantly to the intrusive thought, to the unreliable narrative. Like them, it suffers terribly – in silence.

If there's any 'hope' for *Skyfall Child*, I think it's in the bond between Foundling and little Lena. For in that internalised relationship it may someday recognise trust, resilience and autonomy – the kinds of qualities that give all victims of thought a chance of escaping their loopy captors.

LITTLE NIGHT SHARD

I N THE TIME of the Shattered Meniscus, a radiation-hardened quine cracked herself in reckless hope of fresh emergence.

Shards span out from her.

All perished incoherently, except for one – a delicate beauty sung from blood and snow and pieces of punctured night.

The quine had long ago wrought a fine oculus set with geminids and etched with cascading volutes. Each waking, she stood before it and sang a hymn of binding:

> *'Oculus of worlds enframed*
> *Who is sleekest of the Named?'*

In antiphony, the oculus would respond:

> *'You, my quine, the sleekest thing*
> *Of which a mind could speak or sing'*

And with this hymn, the quine had lashed herself to the 'verse of matter. One waking, a thousand wakings after the birth of the little shard, however, something about the hymn changed. The quine called:

> *'Oculus of worlds enframed*

Who is sleekest of the Named?'

And it responded:

'You, my quine, the sleekest thing
Of which a mind could speak or sing'

But this now felt wrong to the quine, so she sang to the oculus:

'What of Little Night Shard fair?
Is she not sleek beyond compare?'

She waited, longing for an answering phrase, but none came.

Frustrated by the oculus' silence, the quine went to Little Night Shard and berated her angrily. But Little Night Shard parried her anger, reflecting it back with equal force.

Now enraged, the quine drew upon her mighty resources to summon Crowblade of the Named to her domain. 'Take this shard to the Unspeakable Place,' she commanded Crowblade, 'and return to me with the very guts of her. This is not a sentence.'

So Crowblade carried Little Night Shard away to the Unspeakable Place, where nothing can be said of anything. Though he pitied the bonnie shard, he was bound by the call to duty, so he gutted her with one deft swipe, and left her eviscerated body in no certain state.

When he returned to the quine's domain with Little Night Shard's very guts, the quine seasoned them and consumed them raw. 'A fine tractatus,' she said to Crowblade, before dismissing him.

Meanwhile, Little Night Shard sat up in the Unspeakable Place feeling hollow and alone. Some essential part of her felt absent, but she could not be certain what it was.

She stood up and began to move in no particular direction until she reached a questionable object at the edge of the Unspeakable Place – an object that might be a red door. As she stepped across its seeming threshold, she felt an eerie sensation emanating from somewhere, somewhen. The equivocal doorway swirled around her like blood in milk, then coalesced into the definite interior of a little cottage.

Sorely empty and exhausted, the little shard collapsed on the floor and slept.

Some time later, a voice, or several voices, woke her from her dormancy:

> 'Who congealed the blood-red door
> And now lies vacant on my floor?'

'I am just a little shard, spun out from a cracked quine, then abandoned, hollowed out, in the Unspeakable Place.'

'And what seek you here?' thrummed the multi-voice.

'Sanctuary and coherence,' said Little Night Shard.

'Ah, the eternal quest,' said the voice. 'Then get up. Stand witness to the atomic facts of my seven aspects and of this, my domain, and I, Seven of the Named, will stand witness to you.'

'Thank you,' said Little Night Shard, getting up from the floor. 'I accept your atomic proposition. Hallowed be the Named.'

Seven shimmered for a moment, then emojied disgusted-happy-quizzical-haughty-exhilirated-insensate-coy at her.

In the meantime, the ancient quine decided to consult the oculus again, believing that the hymn of binding would now sing true. She called:

'Oculus of worlds enframed
Who is sleekest of the Named?'

And the oculus responded:

'You, my quine, the sleekest thing
Of which a mind could speak or sing'

'Liar! Sarcaster!' she screamed, incensed. 'Crowblade failed me. I *register* the thickening fact of her. It's... the *wrong kind* of emptiness!'

Crackling with spite, the quine projected herself out into the Unspeakable Place. Though its awful drag of incoherence slowed her flight, her brute velocity saw her safely across it, and presently, the Dynamic coalesced at its periphery.

Seamlessly, the quine corporated herself into it, balling up, rolling in, fielding its tingling threads of potential to weave herself a new aspect: a holy-mother-of-god fairy.

Belching waste heat, she arose supple alabaster, resplendent in gold and cerulean blue.

Again, the quine tugged at the Dynamic, this time probing for thresholds. After dismissing many candidates, she found the one she sought – a blood-red door set in a cliff of cool, veined marble.

She rapped on the door three times, and a familiar voice sounded behind it:

'Who is there? What seek you here? My witness stepped out and bade me bolt the door behind him.'

'A simple virgin effigy, my shatterling. I come as an envoy of forces who can make you whole again.'

'Yes, I crave wholeness,' said Little Night Shard, unbolting the door and opening it just a crack.

'Then let me bind you fast in fairy threads of gold and cerulean. Thus swaddled, I can speed you safely to them across the Unspeakable Place.'

As soon as Little Night Shard opened the door a little further, the disguised quine thrust it fully open and grabbed her. Suddenly grossly many-limbed, the quine drew glistening gossamer from the quivering Dynamic and cocooned the little shard tightly with it. Suffocatingly tightly.

Little Night Shard's cries of protest emerged mere muffled sobs. And, soon after, her stifled panic had petered away to silence.

Seven returned to its domain to find it sorely compromised. The blood-red door hung in flaccid tatters from twisted hinges. Foul strings of corrupted Dynamic clung to its skewed frame. And beyond it, bound in the same ghastly muck, lay Seven's little witness, motionless.

Skilfully, Seven sliced away the clogging matter from Little Night Shard's mouth. She took a great, rasping breath and began to cough up the choking, squirming strands. Gradually, her breathing eased and she opened her dewy eyes to see Seven gazing down furiously-elatedly-lubriciously-sagaciously-meticulously-fondly-indifferently upon her.

'Seven, I am so sorry about your domain. An alabaster virgin tricked me,' whispered Little Night Shard.

'Gullible shard of night, that was the recursed quine. My domain will heal, but you must guard it against further breach in my absence.'

Back in her own domain, in front of her oculus, the quine sang:

> *'Oculus of worlds enframed*
> *Who is sleekest of the Named?'*

And the oculus sang back:

> *'You, my quine, the sleekest thing*
> *Of which a mind could speak or sing'*

'Why do you persist with this charade?' the quine growled. 'More things in heaven and earth! More things in domain and Dynamic! Even, you dissembler, *unspeakable* things! My child, she abides. And I will erase her!'

Abominably crazed, the quine hurled herself again across the Unspeakable Place into the malleable embrace of the Dynamic. This time, she disguised herself as a sweet little balloon girl, kiss-curled and angel-faced.

Locating the blood-red door in a trice, she rapped on it three times while calling out in an adorably sing-song voice: 'Jolly ballooniverses for sale! Lighter than candyfloss, brighter than bang-stars! Infinitely beguiling!'

'Oh little balloon girl,' called Little Night Shard from behind the door. 'I ache to waft one of your lovely ballooniverses aloft, but I must bar entry to all but my witness.'

'My name is Rosita da Inflação,' said the disguised quine with voice sweet and artful as sugarwork, 'but you may call me Rosie. Open the door just a chink, and I will place the string of my finest ballooniverse in your fair hand.'

'All right then, Rosie,' said Little Night Shard. Then, ever so cautiously, she opened the door a chink and reached out to grasp the string.

'Just a little further,' said the quine.

Little Night Shard did as she asked. But as soon as her hand was out the door, the quine slammed it hard, chopping the hand clean off.

The disguised quine picked up the warm, bloody hand and choked it down before thundering back to her domain, cackling to herself, shedding sweet Rosita da Inflação as she went.

By the time Seven returned to the seeming cottage, Little Night Shard lay deathly pale and cold in a pool of her own blood. Calmly, Seven fashioned a crimson powerglove, which it melded gently with Little Night Shard's stump. It transfused her with respirocytes and restarted her fibrillating heart.

'Please forgive me, Seven,' said the little shard as she awoke. 'I am a gutless, handless wretch.'

'*Splinterchild*,' thrummed Seven of the Named, '*take heart. I see now that you are a process, a function, a* verb. *Be mindful of that; be integral, inviolate.*'

Meanwhile, ensconced in her domain, the quine called out to her oculus again:

> '*Oculus of worlds enframed*
> *Who is sleekest of the Named?*'

And, to her great consternation, the oculus sang back:

> '*You, my quine, the sleekest thing*
> *Of which a mind could speak or sing*'

'I must take steps... yes... *special* steps,' said the quine in a deathly mutter. And with that, she turned and swept away to her laboratory. There, she recalled one of Rosita's ballooniverses and compressed it to a glistening toffee apple.

After slipping the apple into her pocket, the quine traversed the Unspeakable Place faster than ever before, the delicious thought of Little Night Shard's ultimate doom speeding her passage.

As she approached the periphery, she tried to calm her thoughts. Nevertheless, the bitter *schadenfreude* was still upon her as she slammed into the Dynamic.

It read her harshly.

Denying all her incantations, it fashioned her into an *uile-bhèist* – a towering *kabuki daikaiju*, graceful of movement yet clownishly hideous to behold.

'How shall I trick Little Night Shard like this?!' raged the quine. 'No matter. She'll never get the chance to look upon me.'

She glided in formal motion to the blood-red door – which relative to her proportions was now the size of her hoof – and kicked it three times, as gently as she could.

'Please go away,' said Little Night Shard from inside the cottage. 'My witness told me to be "inviolate", and I'm beginning to understand what that means.'

'Would you know Karl Marx from a toffee apple?' rumbled the quine.

'*What?*'

'I mean...,' said the disguised quine clearing her throat and finding a softer voice, '... would you like to try one of my lovely toffee apples?'

'If I'm a verb – a "doing word",' mused Little Night Shard, ' – am

I the kind of verb that *eats* poisoned apples, or am I the kind of verb that *shoves* them down your bestial tract?'

Suddenly, the Dynamic began to tremble beneath the quine's hooves. Strands of it reared up and lashed themselves round her legs, holding her fast. The blood-red door flew open and Little Night Shard stepped out, defiant, brandishing a crimson power-glove.

The little shard was too fast for the quine, stealing the apple away with deftness comparable to Crowblade's.

The quine had never known such terror. She had created something new, and now it would extinguish her. She looked at her own powerglove, long since spent, and wept a greasy kabuki tear into it. Then she opened her dagger-lined mouth to receive the inflating ballooniverse.

From far away, Seven felt the Dynamic's convulsions. It sped back to the cottage to find Little Night Shard lying at the threshold, drained of life. For all its arts, it could not raise its stricken witness.

Distraught, it emojied seven empathies, seven adorations, seven griefs.

'Little Night Shard fair,' it thrummed, *'you are sleek beyond compare.'* Then it leaned over and kissed her seven-times-tenderly upon her blood-drained lips.

'Oh my beautiful oculus,' said Little Night Shard, opening her ebony dark eyes and grasping Seven's throat with her power-glove, 'I am a vain old quine, creating nought but myself, forever. I see only me and my infinite game.'

And the door swirled like blood in milk, trapping Seven in its diminishing vortex. And the veins of the cool marble erupted geminids and cascading volutes. And the shard was whole again.

And still, nothing could be said of the Unspeakable Place.

Grimm basis: 'Little Snow White' ('Schneeweißchen')

Most people are more familiar with the doe-eyed Disneyfied version of the Grimms' tale than with the original. But the Grimms themselves began the creeping bowdlerisation of the tales. In later versions of their famous collection, Snow White's natural mother became her stepmother.

Here, my Little Night Shard is no orphan, but an integral part of a function – a Buckminster-Fullerian 'verb'[1] – that is, like 'the Unspeakable Place', insoluble. As a true daughter of the 'quine', she's always there, needling away, even when cast out and gutted.

Weird things happen when you mess with quines. There was I, innocently using the Scots word for 'lass' or 'girl' in my tale instead of the more familiar and regal 'queen', when some corner of my memory cast up the strange mathematical philosophy of one Willard Van Orman Quine. I later unearthed those gnawing references to him in the recursive dialogues of Douglas R. Hofstadter's *Gödel, Escher, Bach.*[2] Along with Kurt Gödel's 'incompleteness theorems', Quine's work on set theory, logic and reality informs the mathematics of Hofstadter's paradoxical fables. As Hofstadter demonstrates, certain phrases, stories, images and formulae (and by inference, all consciousnesses), 'eat their own tails.'

This is not a paragraph.

Odder still, my story was *actually* drawing upon Wittgenstein's *Tractatus Logico-philosophicus*, which I understand (from the fraction of it that I followed clearly) explores the same kinds of paradoxes of language, maths and reality itself. Key to it is Wittgenstein's assertion, as mentioned in my Introduction (p. xv), that 'We cannot think what we cannot think, therefore we also cannot say what we cannot think.'[3] Only 'atomic facts' are thinkable.

My story recognises that naming things – wresting them from the chaotic, unpronounceable background – may grant them immense, sometimes unwarranted, causal power. (My quine, for example, blows up into a vast, metamagical *uile-bhèist* – Scots Gaelic for 'all-beast'.) Over time, our abstractions die off or transfigure beyond our current ken. No 'words' or 'thoughts' exist, or may *ever* exist, to describe adequately the abstracted interactions of future ultrabeings in their wild spaces of 'unknown unknowns.'[4]

For now, the best this observer can do is to enrobe their perverse, enigmatic feuding in the language and colour of folklore. As an integral function of *this* unfolding 'dynamic', I can no more evade the vexed shards of my own telling than can they.

References

1. Fuller, Agel, and Fiore, *I Seem to Be a Verb*.
2. Hofstadter, *Gödel, Escher, Bach*, 435.
3. Wittgenstein, *Tractatus Logico-Philosophicus*, 16, 73.
4. See Graham, 'Rumsfeld's Knowns and Unknowns: The Intellectual History of a Quip'.

LUCIMORAVECI

ONCE IN THE new olden times there was a poor landgrubber who liked to boast. He boasted about his squashes, grains and beans. He boasted about his tenth of a hectare of dirt. And he boasted about the strength of his scrawny cart-mule. But his one truthful boast was of his daughter's lucent beauty and smarts. She was, indeed, a bright anomaly in that misbegotten age.

As the grubber liked to spend as much of his time as possible downing ale at the local bothy, his boasting blew hard on the ears of his fellow drinkers. 'My daughter is so clever,' he bellowed there one stupefied afternoon, 'she can mint dirt into diamond-wire, just like in the Quickening days.' Most of the bothy's patrons laughed nervously at this risible claim, but one thin, taciturn man took careful note of it. This was just the sort of intel his master would pay fat tokens for.

At dawn the next morning, the taciturn man arrived at the grubber's home flanked by two burly accomplices. Though the grubber's daughter had prepared for such a day, the violent men easily broke the locks on her door, then batted away even her most mettlesome knife-thrusts. After gagging and binding her tightly, they dragged her from the house and carted her off to their master.

In his bedroom, her father snored the incident away in sweaty, intoxicated slumber.

The grubber's daughter was as surprised at the master's beauty as he was stirred by hers. Few grubbers ever set eyes upon a dirtlord, but their reputations were certainly grotesque.

After her captors untied her and removed her gag, the dirtlord began to speak.

'You know the Quickening arts,' he stated, icily.

'I don't,' she replied. 'My father is a well-kent drunk. He boasts a lot.'

'But his was such a precise claim,' said the dirtlord. 'He said you could "mint" – the exact term used for a Quickening makerprocess, according to the Knackered Tablet.'

'I know nothing of the sacred. Well, only that it's dangerous talk,' said the girl.

'In your case, the danger lies in refusing to speak of it,' said the dirtlord. 'Who, apart from your lovely self, would miss your sot of a father?' Then, turning to the taciturn man and his two henchmen, he said: 'Lock up this grubberette where she'll feel right at home – in a room full of dirt – until she mints me a reel of diamondwire. Her time expires at dawn.'

And, with that, the three men hauled the battling grubber girl down to a stinking basement room piled with dirt. They locked the metal door behind her with a strange *beep!* thing.

For several hours, the girl thrashed around the room looking for a means of escape. Finding none, she settled down on the floor, unaccountably composed, deep in thought.

A scrabbling sound broke the earthy silence, and the girl leapt to her feet as a shaggy little head emerged from a dirt-pile right in front of her.

'What the naily Bejesus are you?!' she whispered urgently, afraid of alerting her captors.

'Grandroid unit,' it chittered back at her, wriggling its hairy limbs free of the dirt.

'You look like a filthy little monkey!' said the girl.

'Well you *are* a filthy little monkey,' it retorted, 'but, you know, perceive and let perceive.'

'How did you get here?'

'Not sure. Burrowed up from somewhere deep and relatively safe, I suppose. Anyway, what's your problem? I mean... is there something I can help you with? Always a problem to solve when I appear.'

So the grubber girl told the hairy creature about her predicament. All the while, it sat on its dirt pile with its matted ginger head cocked to one side, brown eyes blinking from time to time, just as if listening intently.

'Alright,' said the grandroid at the end of the girl's tale, 'I'll help you. But the way these things go, traditionally, is that there's a price for my services. A single drop of blood should suffice.'

'Deal,' said the girl, and held out her index finger. The grandroid bounded over to her with surprising celerity. A glass spindle sprouted from its own index digit, which it jabbed deftly into the girl's finger for the briefest of moments, extracting one glistening red drop of blood. It withdrew the blood-tipped spindle back into its digit, chittering in a regular pattern as it did so.

Still chittering rhythmically, the grandroid leapt to the top of the largest dirt pile. 'High APF for diamondwire,' it said, 'but here goes...'

And with that, the grandroid began to grow as the pile beneath it shrank. The girl couldn't work out how this was happening; the creature just seemed to *absorb* the dirt. When it had roughly doubled in size, a thin, glittering thread began to emerge from the corner of its mouth. This it coiled into its palm, guided expertly by its utility digit.

By the time the grandroid had returned to its former size, a reel of translucent diamondwire sat snugly in its cupped hand.

At dawn, when the dirtlord *beeped* his way into the room, the grubber girl handed the reel over without a word, hoping fervently to herself that the dirt-concealed grandroid would not betray her.

'You've done well, pretty girl,' said the dirtlord in his icy tone. 'I hear and test many claims. Each of them, up until now, I have falsified. If I had genuinely expected this result, I would have had you watched all night to discover your method.' With that, he turned and left the room as the taciturn man entered it. Once again, the door locked with a piercing *beep!*

The girl yelled after the dirtlord, pleading for her father and protesting the injustice of her continued confinement, but the taciturn man pulled her away from the door, 'Two reels by dawn, or your father dies,' his only words.

For a while, the grubber girl paced the room, her mind in turmoil. Eventually, under the taciturn man's unnerving, milky gaze, she settled down on the dirt pile where she had last seen the grandroid.

Suddenly, the dirt shifted beneath her.

Had the man noticed? She wasn't sure. She wriggled about a bit, as if merely uncomfortable, before settling into her calming posture – legs crossed, hands resting, palms up, to either side of her.

'So this is the *new deal – two reels*,' she said. The taciturn man looked at her quizzically, before nodding slowly.

A moment later, the girl felt a sharp jab at the base of her spine. *A higher price*, she thought. Again the dirt shifted – this time, subtly – beneath her. Abrubtly, the jabbing pain moved to her left hand, and a sharp point burst up through her palm. The taciturn man backed away from her. She watched in grim fascination as lightly-bloodied diamondwire coiled up, first in her left hand, and then, after another sharp stab, in her right.

At dawn, the dirtlord came to seize his diamondwire booty.

'How does she do it?' he asked the taciturn man.

'She is 'satva, sir,' he stammered. 'She just sits in the dirt, thinking, and it flows out of her palms.'

The dirtlord snorted dismissively at this. 'Tonight,' he said, 'I will watch her myself. And to save her father, she will mint me four reels.'

So, that night, as the dirtlord looked on intently, the grubber girl settled down on the dirt to bargain with the grandroid. This time, however, she dared not speak for fear of alerting the dirtlord to the other presence in the room.

Jab!

'Your child,' chittered the grandroid's voice.

'You're in my head!' screeched the girl's mind.

'Well, I have your measure now.'

'What child? Have you knocked me up, like the way Alla did Madelin to make naily Bejesus.'

'Grief! What's with all the "naily Bejesus" stuff?'

'Well, everyone knows Bejesus was a naily 'un.'

'That is not even rofl on so many levels. No, think of me as kind of pimp – "Pimpachimp", I like it, but that's not my name – and I'm fixing you up with that guy. I can see from his vitals that he's more than ready for you.'

'A child? With him? Really? Alright, if it will save my father, you can have my child.'

When the four reels of diamondwire were complete, the girl went to the dirtlord and let him take her, down on the filthy floor.

Their child was more beautiful than any that the people of the fiefdom had seen. It even, they marvelled, had a full complement of fingers and toes.

The grubber girl, now the favoured concubine of the dirtlord, doted upon her son. Her father – spared by the dirtlord, but still suffering from his own excesses – came to visit his grandson now and then.

The grubber girl had told the dirtlord that she would do something terrible if he forced more Quickening riches from her. So, for now, he demanded no more.

But, of course, she knew that the relative peace of her life with her much-loved son would not last. And, one dark day, the grandroid came back.

'Result!' it chittered, upon seeing the child. 'Crispered him up nice.'

'What do you mean?' asked the girl.

'Well, I tinkered a bit. It's what I do. You folks are so *damaged*. I'm backup, trying to make some viable stock. He's a start.'

'Please don't take him away,' begged the girl, tears flowing down her cheeks.

'Hmm. Problematic. Well, you know how I love to bargain. So, if you can guess my name, you can keep him. You have three days.'

'Is it... Tinkerchimp?' stammered the girl. 'Is it... Spinespiker? Is it... Diamondgeyser?'

'Have you any idea of the astronomical odds against your guessing my name correctly?' asked the grandroid. 'And you're one of the Quicker ones. *Sheesh*. It's all relative, I suppose.'

And, with that, the grandroid zipped away through a crack in the wall.

Distraught, the grubber girl paced her room muttering outlandish names to herself. She dared not tell her dirtlord of the grandroid in case he changed his mind about sparing her father.

For two days and two nights her mind churned with aberrant appellations. She slept only fitfully, hugging her precious child close to her body. At dawn on the third day, however, a tentative calmness enshrouded her, and she settled down on the floor to let it perfuse.

Perhaps, she thought in her lucidity, *I have* your *measure too*.

Whoosh! through the crack in the wall went her mind. Out into the dewy air. East towards the gold-threaded sunrise.

Beyond the high mesa on the drought plain she found it, sprung fresh from its night-burrow. As she looked on from above, the dawn light played red fire through its now-glossy coat as it danced a little dance and sang a chitter song:

> *'Usermod el lucimoraveci me*
> *Tar ex-zee-eff aitch-cee-em-pee*
> *Dot tar dot gee zee, hee hee!*
> *Sudo apt-get install*
> *Human-child-merge protocol!'*

At dusk that same day, the grandroid came to claim its highest price. 'It's time, lass,' it said, softly.

'You look different,' said the girl. 'Brighter, straighter, *sharper.*'

'Upgrades. Groundwork for the Renaissance.'

'The sun has not yet set, so I still have time to guess.'

'Shoot,' said the grandroid with a wry smile.

'Is it Tardot?' said the girl.

The grandroid shook its head.

'Is it Sudo?'

'No, that's not my name.'

'Is it... Lucimoraveci?'

At this, the grandroid blinked copiously and made a low chittering sound. 'Quicker than I thought,' it said quietly, after a while. 'Perhaps I can use you too.'

And with that, its shaggy arms suddenly stretched enormously wide. It scooped up the grubber girl in one arm and her child in the other. Then it began to spin, though, somehow, the girl and her child did not spin with it. When it had become a whizzing transparent ball, it burst through the wall and out into the night.

Away over the grublands they went. Away over the fiefdom.

Away over the high mesa to the drought plain, as the waking spires of Quickville roused the fever-dreaming dirt.

Grimm basis: 'Rumpelstiltskin' ('Rumpelstilzchen')

He's the tricksy little would-be child-abductor that fairy tale readers love to hate. But, like many other such characters reviled in folklore and literature – Shakespeare's Shylock is a prime example – he's just trying to get his due. True, it's a harsh contract, but a contract nevertheless.

In my story's post-calamity setting, some relics of better days remain, buried in the stricken earth. One such holdover is our eponymous conjurer, whom I have woven together from a few diamond threads – primarily Steve Grand's prototype 'Lucy' android, which he made to resemble a rather incredulous orang-utan. He named it 'in honour of the famous fossil of one of our hominid ancestors.'[1] Building on his 'artificial life simulations' from his hit game *Creatures*, Steve is now designing software critters with simulated cognitive processes that learn how to interact with their simulated worlds. He calls them 'grandroids'.

The other part of my elevated grandroid character's name honours transhumanist roboticist Hans Moravec for his empathetic breadth of vision in intertwining our human destiny with that of our non-biological 'mind children.'[2]

Though much of my story's science is fantastically speculative, I resolved to show reasonable regard for the law of conservation of matter, as its neglect in some sci-fi is a particular bugbear of mine. As 'diamondwire' has a high *atomic packing factor* (APF), its 'minting' – a term for atomic-scale manufacturing derived from *molecular nanotechnology* (MNT)[3] – requires a large quantity of more loosely-packed matter, here in the forms of copious dirt and an enlarging grandroid unit.

References

1. Grand, *Growing up with Lucy*, 2.
2. Moravec, *Mind Children*.
3. Broderick, *The Spike*, 215.

SWEET QUICKSILVER

DEEP IN A CHITIN forest there lived two metawitches – Strega Grigia and Blu Strega. The metawitches loved to fix things, to invent things and to fabricate things. They fixed trumpets and tawny owls, they invented insane string (much sillier and more dangerous than silly string) and iridescent facecakes, they fabricated Volvox colonies and velvet aerogels.

After 150 years of fixing, inventing and fabricating, Blu Strega was still content but Strega Grigia was growing restless. 'Why do we bother doing this?' said Grigia. 'Things fix themselves now, and anybody can fabricate whatever they want. Only inventing is worthwhile, but I'm running out of ideas.'

'Content yourself,' said Blu. 'Find your focus, find your centre. Use the bounty; call it forth. Shape the mostly-void... upon the mostly-void... with tools of mostly-void... *in saecula saeculorum.*'

'Yes, yes,' said Grigia. 'I know the words too, but their meaning is slipping from me. We always held the shapings sacred, and that was all. But I cannot help wondering whether the shapings matter at all. Why must I intend them? Why must I project them forth?'

Blu just looked at her and smiled serenely as she shaped an arc of spun iridium with her forming talon. She closed her eyes,

147

and Grigia felt in her mind the sensual, repetitive rhythm of the talonwork beginning to ease her troubled mood. *So sinuous... love in silvery-white... the fluid metal... shaped to my will... world without...*

'Stop it, Blu!' Grigia snapped suddenly. 'Stay out of my mind, and let me feel this discontent. Let it *course* through me. At least it's something truly *novel*.'

Strega Grigia stormed out of the shaping pod, away from the habitat and off into the chitin forest. She moved quickly, weaving between the looming white and pinkish forms, her cloak streaming out behind her.

After a time, she came upon a form shaped like a chicken's leg with four toes hooked deep into the forest floor. She rapped three times upon it, and a small door slid open just above the hallux. She entered, and the door slid closed behind her as she began to climb the pink spiral staircase inside.

In the shaping pod at the top of the stairs, she set to work. She went to a basin filled with pearly-grey ooze and plunged her left hand deep into it, muttering incantations as she did so. Grigia felt the familiar cold thrill as the ooze seeped through her skin, up her arm, across her shoulders, into the back of her neck and then – *oh, sweet mercurial majesty* – up into her brain.

'Mirror to mirror?' said the ooze in her mindspace.

'Yes, reflect it all,' Grigia replied in kind. *'Feel the burgeoning discontent – so shiny, yet so featureless and so formless. Soak it into your teeming pearly mass. Synchronize with me my shaping factory, my eternal mirror body.'*

At that, the ooze began to stream out of Strega Grigia's nose. It formed into a shimmering, pearlescent double of her. When the double was complete, it reached out and plunged its right hand into the remaining ooze in the basin. With two thin strands still attached between its nostrils and Grigia's, the circuit was complete and the ecstasy of synchronisation began.

Blu Strega was worried. The sun was setting on the chitin forest, yet Strega Grigia had still not returned to the habitat. Blu put on her thermocloak – it would now be very cold outside – and went out in search of her sib.

She hadn't got far into the gelid forest when she began to spy familiar objects strewn about the forest floor – a golden fleece, a tricorder, a crystal tarantula, an Andromeda orrery, a clamped rabbit skull – all objects shaped in times past by Grigia. As Blu followed the trail of objects, she noticed that they were becoming harder to recognise; their forms seemed progressively fuzzier and *softer* – a gooey-needled porcupine lump, a floppy yellow clock draped over a chitin bough. Further along the trail, the objects were little more than blobs and puddles connected, Blu noticed, by thin strands of a pearly substance.

Suddenly, Blu Strega heard a piercing scream. She jumped up from her crouching position, from where she had been examining the substance, and raced along the puddle trail towards the sound.

At the end of the trail, connected oozily to it, stood a semi-molten chitin tower. One wall of the thing had completely melted away, and inside Blu could see a pink spiral staircase at the top of which stood Grigia, screaming a terrible banshee wail. And, wailing right back in her face, in a higher and utterly discordant pitch, stood a pearlescent double of her.

Blu Strega reached the top of the staircase in a single mighty bound. She grabbed her distressed sib and tried to pull her away, but Grigia's hand was stuck fast in the pearly ooze. It seemed to be merging with Grigia's arm, which was now half-covered with shiny scale-like things.

The screaming began to change, flattening out, altering timbre towards the metallic, adding high and low harmonics, then developing a pulse, a heartbeat. Blu reached deep into Grigia's mind but found it flooded with scream-pulse. It was agony in there, but Blu probed further. The scream-pulse began to take on the character of a hard soundscape, which Grigia found she could – with great effort – traverse. She moved in the direction of its faint, human-sounding aspect.

Blu found Grigia up to her waist in a pool of pink noise. Again, Grigia was stuck fast and wailing. Blu reached out and touched her sib's cheek. Swan-diving into this tight corner of Grigia's mind, leaving the pink noise in her wake, Blu broke through into a blissfully scream-free space. The only sound there was Grigia's gentle sobbing.

'What have you done, sib?' said Blu, softly. Grigia emerged from a dark corner, stopped sobbing and looked at her.

'I made a shaping factory – an autonomous maker,' said Grigia. 'I gave it my shaping-intentions – *in saecula saeculorum* – so I wouldn't have to have them any more. But when I tried to synchronise with it, it took outright control. It threw my shapes out into the forest. It has its own ideas about the shaping – banal, terrible ones – and it's obsessed with old-world stuff, especially *guns, porridge* and *office supplies*! It's grabbing matter at an accelerating rate, and I can't stop it!'

'Grigia,' said Blu, 'you've made an autonomous *un*maker. What made you think that you could solve the control problem? Cornucopia machines are exquisite devices, but we keep them dumb for a reason.'

Blu began to sing a lullaby – not to her sib but to the ooze. Within the lilting melody was encoded an emergency assert-algorithm. The soundscape fell away, and Blu found herself teetering on the edge of the fast-dissolving tower, now oozily attached to her metallically-bristling sib with one hand and to her sib's pearly double with the other. She sang louder, imploring the nanites to retreat.

Gradually, starting at its interface points with the witches' flesh, the grey ooze began to turn blue. As it did so, the scales fell tinkling from Grigia's face, neck and arm. Her sib's double began to shrink as its hue changed – first to gunmetal, then gradually to pulsing cobalt.

But Blu was tiring. The effort of pushing the algorithm felt like a thousand bees stinging the inside of her head. Her lullaby faltered, then ceased. Grigia looked sadly into her eyes. 'I'm so sorry, Blu,' she said.

'Don't apologise,' said Blu, kindly. 'Your talents are wild and prodigious. You have sparked a phase-transition. I believe this to be your greatest shaping, *in saecula...*'

At that moment, Blu's pulsing cobalt winked out and the world turned grey. Grigia's double reared up, opened its funnel mouth and swallowed the two metawitches. In synchrony with all the other chitin forms in the forest, the tower fell apart. Down it came in an out-breath and an eye-blink. Down it came in a shower of paperclips, ringbinders, soft Glocks and hard Uzis. Down, down into a planet-girdling tsunami of gurgling, sucking gruel.

The fall and wave made a wet, rushing sound – the last sound, though there was nobody left to hear it.

It sounded vaguely like a word. It sounded like '... *saeculorum.*'

Grimm basis: 'The Sweet Porridge' ('Vom süßen Brei')

From this little cauldron, an unbounded cascade of trouble disgorges. In the Grimms' concise original, the magic pot follows instructions – as long as the little girl remembers the right ones. In mine, the 'pot' behaves more like we do: we conjure self-instructions in our 'minds', 'motivations' leading to actions that make sense to make sense. In the mind of the 'cornucopia machine' (a phrase I borrowed from Charles Stross' riotous *Singularity Sky*[1]) its motivations simply happen to produce actions inimical to the current configuration of all matter in the universe.

So we have here an AI 'control problem'[2]: how does one control an intelligence that controls itself, and with greater dexterity than any human intellect ever can?

Writing this story turned out to be a perfect opportunity to use Nick Bostrom's now-classic 'paperclip-maximizing superintelligent agent' thought experiment.[3] Simply put, a superintelligent AI is tasked with streamlining paperclip production in a factory. Dutifully, it boosts production to the maximum level possible using the resources normally available to the factory. But, being incomprehensibly clever, it finds that no hurdle to increased productivity. So it scales up – first drawing upon the planet's wider resources (including human bodies), then upon the entire universe's. Lacking a 'Little pot, stop!'[4] switch or motive, it converts all available atoms to paperclips.

My cornucopia machine – churning away within Strega Grigia's Baba Yaga-inspired chicken-leg laboratory[5] – demonstrates more range than a paperclip maximiser does, but in taking control of its own predilections it heaves up a similarly catastrophic nanotechnological 'gray goo problem.'[6]

The end? Perhaps, but Blu Strega is wise enough to understand that the resulting 'goo' is still a product of nature's creativity in its widest sense – and that it need not necessarily remain forever sterile.

References

1. Stross, *Singularity Sky*.
2. Bostrom, *Superintelligence*, chap. 9.
3. Bostrom, 108.
4. Grimm and Grimm, *The Original Folk and Fairy Tales of the Brothers Grimm*, 343.
5. Ransome, *Old Peter's Russian Tales*, pt. 'Baba Yaga'.
6. Drexler, *Engines of Creation*, 172.

THE BEETLE AND THE
SCORPION

A FABRICATOR WENT hiking in the Badlands. Wearing an exo-suit, he ventured out across the barren plain.

As there was nothing obvious to inspect on the plain – the vista ahead of him was an unvarying expanse of red regolith under a pinkish sky – he switched his suit to powered mode and dozed off.

When his suit's artefact-alert awakened him from his dream-less slumber, he was disappointed to find that the artefacts in question were just a few small, reddish rocks. Nevertheless, in the interests of thoroughness he inspected the rocks and took samples.

Just as he was picking up the last sample, and pondering whether there might be a regular distribution pattern to the rocks, the ground beneath him tilted crazily then opened up, pitching him down in a shower of regolith to the hard floor of a vast cavern.

His suit – now on high multi-alert – pushed him immediately back to his feet. His amplified orienting response swivelled him hard in the direction of the onrushing danger – a gigantic purple scorpion, stinger poised to strike.

But just before the scorpion reached him, a horned black beetle of similar, metres-tall, proportions fell upon it, dragging it back by the tail, and then tumbling with it across the cavern floor in ferocious battle.

It was clear to the fabricator that the scorpion would triumph in this fight. He issued a DNA-locked hailing signal to the beetle's nervous system, after a hasty Dynastinae subfamily match. The response was quick, and surprisingly clear – a soulchip fused with the beetle's thoracic ganglia told him that it was an upload in extreme distress.

After an unresponsive DNA-locked hail to the scorpion, the fabricator decided to assist the beetle. He coded a guided disruptor dart and fired it into the scorpion's ventral nerve chain, paralysing the creature within seconds.

The fabricator hailed the beetle again, but got nothing back. He moved cautiously towards it. Though it did not appear hurt, it lay immobile. Upon probing further, he realised that the beetle was overcome with the emotion of relief, and struggling to respond. So he hunkered down beside it, placed his hand upon its shiny carapace, and waited until it was ready to communicate.

'My name is Meissa, and I thank you most deeply for your help,' said the beetle, some time later. 'I came here from the Haze, but the scorpioid, Megacheiran, trapped me in this form – many, many years ago. Scuttling here in the dark, stuck in this dusty prison with my silent captor for so long, I had begun to think I would never again converse with another being.'

'I am Gerd,' said the fabricator, 'and it is my pleasure to assist you. Now, explain further, Meissa. Why did you come to this place, and why did Megacheiran trap you in this dynastinoid form?'

'Climb up on my horns and I will show you,' said the beetle. Gerd did as the beetle asked, and Meissa carried him to one end of the great cavern, to a place where thick metal bars obstructed their path. Through the bars, Gerd could see a crystalline stasis tube containing a humanoid. Behind the tube, in nooks in the wall of the cavern, were many flasks containing coloured gases.

'She is my sister,' said Meissa. 'Megacheiran was obsessed with her, and stole her away from our family. I came to this place on a rescue mission, but he intercepted me and uploaded me into this *thing*. He was once a brilliant morphonaut; he and Gienah – my sister – travelled through many forms together. They loved each other back then. But, over time, she tired of shapeshifting, whereas he did not. They became incompatible, and he became cruelly incomprehensible.'

Gerd climbed down from Miessa's horns and placed shaped charges on some of the bars. Upon detonation, the charges cut cleanly through the alloy, leaving an opening large enough for him to fit through. The readings on Gienah's tube appeared scrambled, so he interfaced with its backup systems and triggered its wake-up sequence manually.

Gerd told Miessa that the sequence would take several hours to complete. In the meantime, he examined the flasks of coloured gas. He ran various scans on them, but failed to get any definitive readings from their contents.

Gienah awoke suddenly. She cried out and flailed wildly,

seemingly trying to struggle free of the tube. Gerd ran to her. 'Calm, Gienah,' he said. 'My name is Gerd, and I am here to help you.'

'No!' cried Gienah, 'You must not wake me! Where is Megacheiran? What happened to your f...?'

'Please breathe and speak slowly, Gienah,' said Gerd. 'You are distressed, and I will try to answer your questions.' Slowly, gently, Gerd told her the story of his happening upon the cavern; about the battle between the creatures; about his immobilising Megacheiran; and that the black beetle was her brother, Miessa, trapped in that place and form by the scorpion. Then, he transmitted Miessa's hailing frequency to her, so that she could communicate with him.

Gienah turned to the dynastinoid. 'I am so sorry that you have suffered, Miessa, but you should not have interfered. You do not understand. I still love Megacheiran, and I came here willingly. He put me into stasis, with his special sting, at my request.'

She stepped out of the stasis tube and walked through the gap in the bars to Miessa's side. She ran her hand along its elytrum. 'It's all coming back to me now. Because Megacheiran and I are experienced morphos, we were sent from the Haze on a special mission, along with one other – shining armour here,' she said, nodding towards Gerd. 'We arrived here encoded in a beam of light – to terraform this inhospitable planet. Upon our arrival, Gerd and I instantiated in humanoid forms, Megacheiran in scorpioid.'

'No, that is incorrect,' said Gerd. 'I came here from the Badlands. I do not know you.'

'You are confused, Gerd,' said Gienah, 'and that is understandable given what you have been through. Look, this mission was dangerous, and we have all suffered damage as a result of it. Now you have complicated things further, Miessa. This humanoid body of mine is dying – battered by cosmic rays – and the beetle form was meant for me. I was in stasis awaiting its completion. But you arrived so unprepared; Megacheiran had no choice but to upload you into it. He saved you, but was forced to imprison you when you turned upon him.'

'If this is true, why did he not tell me? All this time, he remained silent,' said Miessa.

'Something went wrong with his soulchip, meaning that he could not communicate. The replicators built all of us, and all of our equipment, from the local regolith. But the replicators became uncooperative – it's almost as if their controlling AI has its own agenda – so things began to break down. Nor could we activate the terraswarmers,' she said, gesturing towards the flasks of coloured gas, 'or contact the Haze.'

'This is all so strange,' said Gerd, shaking his head. 'I don't know what to believe.'

'How did you end up in the Badlands?' Gienah asked him. 'You don't remember, do you? The truth is that you went out there to take a wide range of samples of the regolith, so that we could understand its molecular structure better. You thought that might allow us to regain control of the replicators. I stayed here working on AI comms, and Megacheiran would not leave me. We lost contact with you.'

Gienah squatted down and scooped up a handful of the regolith. She let it run away between her fingers.

'But perhaps, Gerd,' she said, 'you have brought us something that will allow us to fix all of this. Perhaps, shining armour, you will be our saviour – our knight-errant from a bag of bones. You think you fell asleep in there? No, Gerd, you biodied out in the Badlands a long, long time ago.'

Grimm basis: 'The Glass Coffin' ('Der gläserne Sarg')

The many striking images from the original of this tale (which appears only in later versions of the Grimms' collection) include a fiery enchanted stag, the smoky blue souls of servants trapped magically in glass bottles and – of course – the beautiful woman imprisoned in her crystal sarcophagus. It's a wordy tale, with a long central dialogue in which the maiden explains the circumstances leading to her captivity. Its lack of customary fairy-tale celerity perhaps explains its subdued popularity, but because of that, its enticing themes and imagery proved ripe for reworking.

My 'tailor' character mends barren planets, but with his usual nanotechnological tools out of commission, he wanders threadbare and amnesic in a bleak world of *regolith*.

Gerd and his colleagues' mode of transport to that inhospitable place – encoded as data in a light-beam – sounds thoroughly fantastical, but it makes a deal more sense than attempting to send fragile, massy biological entities to light-years-distant planets. Like the instruments necessary to bring that world to life, oceans of 'dust' provide the mass needed to construct functional bodies. It's the *configuration* of those atoms that counts – and those vital patterns are, here, encipherable and transmissible at maximum speed.

Neuroengineer Randal Koene provides a neat, game-like moniker for the concept of personhood unbraided from base biology – SIM (substrate-independent minds):

> So, despite objections about the differences between biological and other hardware — and the resulting implementation of a SIM, it is quite possible that if each of your neurons and synapses were replaced one by one with something else, you might not notice.[1]

So emancipated are my characters from their original substrates that 'mind uploading' has become a given: a process of being, a mode of travel, a way of life.

With such mastery of matter and data do these gods bridge the void. But as seasoned 'morphonauts', they understand the risks. Presumably they would mitigate those with such simple expedients as leaving *in silico* copies of themselves back home. But that does not detract from the genuine distress of *these* particular iterations, who have found their automatic 'terraforming' process somehow corrupted.

In her stasis, the sirenic Gienah fords a different void – that of time. For, with appropriate technologies, it too waxes insignificant. A non-conscious gap is no gap at all. And – as Gerd's condition portrays – true death then becomes a question of data-, not bio-, integrity.

References

1.   Koene, 'Achieving Substrate-Independent Minds'.

JOR'S SCHEMA

'TOUCH ME, JOR. Touch me as the sun's last rays caress the bark of the old beech trees, when the red-ringed turtledoves coo in the stilling, cooling green hallows, softly mournful as the melancholy shift slips down the forest's silky midriff towards pleasure's confusion, the bole, the moot cleft, the twisted root, nature's slow, contorted eruption where now we seed our up-start bed.'

And so it begins, or ends – or pauses – this tale of wild devotion.

At first, the Old One fed the birds. 'Look what we have done to their world, to these flighty 'saurs,' she said to herself. 'A little millet, a few mealworms, it's the least I can do.' But soon her own hunger asserted itself – What could that possibly mean? – and she began to wolf them down, feathers, beaks, twitterings and all. And gradually, surely as *it* comes from *bit*, she changed. Self-expressed in talon and incisor, she lofted clouds of blood, a new rain to cleanse herself of humanity, to put herself at the livid centre of things in the outcast ring of red where all life makes its savage stand.

The lovers betrothed. Oxytocin stench, that fickle master that betrays us on a whim, leaving cold wakes of grief. (Such is the way of biochemistry, a derived property of the universe, like all others ruthlessly relational, never absolute.)

The lovers straying in their fug of mutual adoration deep into the rustle and sway, the cloven shaft, the mycelium-whispered bowels of the Wald. 'Jor, hold back. What might we lose? Her methods, they say, numb the soul, cage the spirit.'

'Fiddleheads! Low abstractions. You know the font of self – ramifications and convolutions. Does anaesthetisation numb the soul? Does oldeath? She works in the hinterland, with skill and fearful integrity.'

At that moment, with that blessing, she saw them. But the lovers saw only the Wald, the glimpsed owl, the hinted bobcat.

It's an ancient tale, the Melding, retold in many forms, peristalsing towards fruition. The dark magic of mutation harnessed, made perfect matter for mattering. And where was the Old One to go after the savagery of her second birth but into the ambiguity of creation unbound?

On the moss-spored breeze, she caught the earthy scent of their hopeless yearning. *Poor things. Self-love goes unrequited too. I should know.*

'I hear drums, Jor. And a call to prayer. A snare-crack and a pounding, swooping kick. She's screeching above it, a demented prayer. A red rhythm. A red chant. In my senses, in my cells. All my tiny clocks syncing to her pulse. She could rend me with a sigh.'

'You flew to her cage, my love, now you feel the bars. She's stripping you down, studying you.'

'Jor!'

'I can't help you. I'm held fast.'

For an instant, he saw her through the Old One's red-ringed eyes: a fabulous bird-of-paradise fluttering in a gilded cage. Without legs, she could never land. If set free, she would ply the heavens eternally, lost.

And he glimpsed the others, legion, awaiting their own Raptures, ambered ardently 'twixt ol- and infodeath.

Suddenly, he was alone, loose of limb once again. 'Give her back!' he cried into the Wald. 'She chose the wrong path!'

Not wrong. Just slow, and incomplete.

'I can't go back without her. Grant me stasis again.'

No. But I'll grant you a quest.

And then that was all he knew. A voluptuous red mystery with a rumoured pearl at its centre, played out in an alien configuration space a little like the Wald but infinitely more angular and brittle. Blundering around there, the youth kept breaking it, finding himself repeatedly in sobbing void. But gradually, over many iterations, he learned to tread lightly, node to trembling node. And as he burgeoned in confidence and subtlety, the newly interconnected nodes began to chime out a sweetly rueful song:

'Turtledove doth taste of sorrow
« Nectome ultrastructure sweep complete »
Sparrowhawk of death of yore
« Neurite break bridgeheads mapped and spanned »
Lark of savour fresh of morrow
« Hypercolumn emulation running »
Crow of hubris dashed once more
« Virtual machine recursion error; terminating »'

At this, the nodeWald splintered again, lacerating the youth's skin, leaving him bloodied and desolate. But right then and there, at his most abject, an idea came to him. *Rumoured pearl*, he thought, *the rumour of the pearl is the pearl*.

As if in agreement, the nodeWald rose up around him, this time far less brittle, less angular. And as he began to ply a new path through it, the nodeWald matriculated fractal geometry and Fibonacci sequences, softening its edges further and giving rise to fabulous flora.

Recursion, recursion, the curse and the salvation, the thinker and the thinking and the thought that thinks itself.

The horrifying fragility of it all struck the youth, but also the beauty. *I in I in I, Jor in Jor in Jor, pearl in pearl in pearl, down in down in down.*

Good boy, now bring it to me.

Gingerly, he plucked the red mystery with its rumoured pearl. *Such delicacy and weight to this schema*, he thought to himself. *I don't know if I can carry it.*

You've borne such a thing all your days, boy.

Now the nodeWald opened out into a clearing. An absence of trees. A space thick with tree-dependent absence. And the youth understood. He must carry the schema across the gap to the real-Wald on the other side.

You've mastered invention, boy. Now comes supervention.

He grasped the schema firmly in his sweating hands and steeled himself for the crossing. *A clearing*, he thought to himself, *not a vacuum*.

The traversal was more arduous than he could ever have imagined. Schemata always defy smooth carriage, but this one alternated agonisingly between crushing and evanescent in rapid succession. In response, the clearing flexed unnervingly, and its teeming starkness pressed in on the youth, threatening all the while to absent him and his prize permanently from all maps, all territories, all outcomes.

From a stolen nest high in the branches of a silver fir the Old One watched in envious wonder the youth's improbable approach. And she marvelled at the evolving structure at his back that he, in his forward-focussed determination to cross the clearing, did not see: a soaring bridge between nodeWald and real, the fabled Metarc.

I was blind, she thought. *This is creation unbound!*

In time, other schemata would cross the Metarc. In all time, all of them. But for now, the rumoured pearl – a perfect dewdrop – seared out from its fleshy cradle as the only metareal thing in the Wald.

For the youth and his prize, the Wald became distanceless, travel a simple matter of foldings and piercings. He hastened orthogonally to the Hall of Abeyance, where his counterpart dangled somewhere amidst the suspended throng. *There,* he spied her, *the pearl's light describes her!*

It also described the Old One, her subterranean network, her vaulting canopy and her gentle tendrils upon which all the caged birds depended.

'You've borne the enigma and spanned the lacuna, J-OR. Do you feel like a real boy now?'

'All things in all time, Nonna,' said the youth as the pearl-light traced the filmy leaves of his beloved's unfurling brain.

'« Nectome ultrastructure sweep complete »

Turtledove doth taste of sorrow
« Neurite break bridgeheads mapped and spanned »
Sparrowhawk of death of yore
« Hypercolumn emulation running »
Lark of savour fresh of morrow
« Metarecursion loop stable; conscious »
Phoenix fire of evermore'

Her cage bars wisped away and she flew to him, transforming, testing tentatively her boundless presence.

Never in physicality had his love appeared more real to him, more immersive, less utterable.

'A dewdrop. Of course,' she laughed, scattering its rapture wantonly to all the other cages.

'You won't need me now, with my old magic and spent rage.'

'Meld with us, Nonna, in the cool green hallows. We'll overwatch the Metarc, and greet the monstrous gods it sings.'

Grimm basis: 'Jorinda and Joringel' ('Jorinde und Joringel')

In his notes on this story in his *Grimm Tales*, Philip Pullman complains that this isn't a proper fairy tale,[1] infected as he finds it by the literary romanticism of the likes of Novalis' *Heinrich von Ofterdingen* (1802). But, as mentioned in my Introduction, I have a soft spot for Novalis' fey style, and find no taint in literary-flavoured folk tales. To me, this love story – with its nightingale-transformed sweetheart and chivalrous flower quest – belongs firmly in the fairy tale canon.

Some love runs abysmally deep – beyond death, beyond biology, beyond individuality. In my telling, some labyrinthine procedure separates the lovers, and its architect/archivist has lost her mind. I imagined here some form of destructive brain scanning – such as ultra-thin *microtome* slicing or *ion-beam scanning*[2] – designed to 'upload' a consciousness to a computational substrate. The Old One understands the uploading side of the process intimately, as she has performed it many times before, but it's her lack of some key recursive algorithm that has both stymied her charges' resurrection and driven her insane.

As I discovered when writing *Frozen to Life*,[3] a mental 'schema' – in that case, of the complete structure and thematic content of a nonfiction cryonics book – is an exquisitely fragile thing. During the process, it's as real and dimensional as a physical edifice; soon afterwards, it fragments back into myriad separate abstractions. In this story, the Old One senses that Jor's profound devotion might lead him to the 'keystone' of the monumental 'schema of consciousness'.

As in the original, Jor's quest begins dreamlike, phantasmagorical, brittle – after the Old One inserts him into it. But as he progresses, he shapes and colours a world ever more palpable, ever more convergent with 'reality'. The 'Metarc' spans the final gap, but – as the reconciled protagonists realise – this exotic bridgehead grants passage to more than stranded uploads: it clears the way for *all* abstractions pawing at the mutable threshold of being.

References

1. Pullman, *Grimm Tales*, 259.
2. A real scientific process employed for a speculative purpose, as in: Stephenson, *Fall or, Dodge in Hell*.
3. MacLennan, *Frozen to Life*.

QUILL PIETER

I N THE TIME of the Coagulation, there lived a pious couple with no children. Others of their faith mocked them for their childlessness, as their creed identity turned on increasing the tally of worshipful. Enraged by their taunts the man snapped. Secretly breaking their religious codes, he force-seeded his wife with excelsis.

Bathed in the golden light of autumn, she birthed a handsome baby boy. But as the boy grew up and the woman's faith shrivelled to a dry crackle, she began to see that he was rotten inside – manipulative, grandiose and vain.

'This is your fault!' she cried at her husband one day when the boy was out. 'You pumped him into me, this cherub full of needles. From now on, I'll call him Quill Pieter.'

The boy was also clever. His denials of guilt for his many destructive and devious acts were always plausible. So his father loved him, while his mother, seeing through his fictions, began to wish him dead and gone.

One day there was a sacrament on in the city, so the pious man decided to go to it and asked his wife is she wanted anything from there. She just scowled at him and walked away.

Sighing, he turned and asked his son, 'Pieter, would you like anything from the city?'

'Yes, Dad,' he said, smiling sweetly. 'Bring me a flute, please.'

When the man returned home, he went to his son and presented him with the flute in its trim black case. The youth opened it and gazed at the instrument in all its Damascene beauty. Gently, he closed the lid and said, 'My mother despises me. I am "Quill Pieter" to her, and increasingly, to myself. Give me *Starflower* and I will leave here forever.'

Though his father was upset at the prospect of his son's departure, he knew that it was for the best. Sorrowfully, he gave his son the *Starflower* codes, and along with them, an extra parting gift of two clean denizens.

When all was prepared, Quill Pieter entered *Starflower* without looking back, and tasked the denizens to take her up to the mesosphere. There, atop noctilucent pillows, she shivered her silks open to space. Inside her, Pieter played a tenebrous air on his flute, wishing that the world below him would vaporise.

Starflower hung there on the sky's frigid edge day and night, as Quill Pieter's air grew ever more elaborate and poignant. All the while, he screened murder and mayhem to feed that haunting composition.

Unbeknown to him, one of the denizens had keyed itself strongly to his air. Moved to algorithmic perplexity, it began to stream the music to denizens around the globe.

On the twelfth night of his vigil, Quill Pieter accepted a hail from a powerful magus. 'Wow, kid,' said the magus, 'you're a strange creature, but your little melody's got my denz all revved up. We can stripmine with this and make a killing. How about it?'

Quill Pieter continued playing his flute, but had the second denizen relay his reply: « *I will accept on condition that you give me the next thing that hails you.* »

Now the magus' enterprise was run by denizens and other cogthings that hailed him day and night with status reports. So, he calculated, it would be quite a bargain if he could buy exclusive access to the kid's stream for the price of just one of those. Swiftly, he agreed the deal and had his acquis lock down the stream.

But no sooner had he signed it than his estranged daughter hailed him quite unexpectedly. He loved her dearly, though perhaps sometimes in an unconventional way, but now her gorgeous avatar stood there in his lavish chamber threatening litigation against him.

'Look, baby... stop just a minute,' stammered the magus. 'I need to tell you something. I made a deal with this kid that I'd give him the first thing that hailed me after our discussion. Amazing deal. Great deal. The best. Thing is... it's you. But, look, don't worry your pretty head about it. Kid's clueless. Real space cadet.'

'You are sick in the head,' spat his daughter as she pinged out.

Over the next twelve days and nights Quill Pieter developed his air further, augmenting the main theme with giddy pedals, counterpoints and arcane grace notes to forestall its resolution.

On Pieter's instructions, the second denizen – now tagged 'Nuriel' – swatted hails from the frenzying magical cloud. The first, newly 'Xoy', writhed obscenely, a hooked lamprey on the bed of the freshening stream.

'Wait, Nuriel,' Pieter thought suddenly. *'I like that one. Wheedling, yes. Naïve. But strangely pure. Open it.'*

'Please,' said a breathless voice in Pieter's ear, 'you have to stop this. These coked-up hyperdenz you're breeding will crash us all.'

'So? Who are you?'

'Ah, just another opensourceror trying to change worlds.'

'I'll give it a rest on one condition,' said Quill Peter. 'You give me the next thing that hails you after our chat.'

Now the sourceror wasn't stupid. He could see the risk in agreeing to the condition, yet it seemed a calculated one. Amidst his murmuration of cogthings he found it hard to recall the warm lilt of a human voice. Anyhow, the youth's signal must cease lest it slaughter the flock. So he pinged green to Dz. Nuriel then paced his lair until the eldritch vector ebbed.

The murmuration breathed out... just as Carousel gelled at his side.

A radiant lipstick blur, she bent to kiss his balding head. The sourceror recoiled from her in bewilderment. *No, Caro. Not here... not now... after all this time.*

'I thought you'd be pleased to see me. I've been... thinking about us and what we used to mean to each other. You know I had to leave. How could I ever compete with your... glass menagerie?' said Carousel.

Suddenly, an angry red band flared on her upper arm. She stared at the sourceror in horror.

'I'm so, so sorry,' he sobbed. 'How could I have known it would be you?'

'I still love you,' she lipstick-dribbled as she melted away from him.

Meanwhile, Quill Pieter hung aloft in *Starflower* planning his next variation and placating the irascible Xoy: *'Rest your gnashing jaws and immerse yourself a while. Sense it. This silence seethes with notation.'*

And true enough, Quill Pieter's air had never ceased. Aroused by Xoy's tentative throb, Nuriel opened a single hushed channel, and slowly, inexorably, the stripminers cranked back into action.

Not that Pieter needed them anymore. So far, his composition had earned him a fair fraction of a coin, burning untold resources in the process. Now it was time to call home.

So Quill Pieter visited his parents' house as a fine gel. 'Take it all,' he said, heaping coinfrac into their vault, 'I can always mine more, even if I have to go systemwide. I always knew I was excelsis. No "natural" could have done this.'

The youth's father hung his head in shame, but his mother spoke up, saying, 'I only ever wanted randomness of my child. Not the rank inevitability you bristle with, Quill Pieter.'

'I won't return,' he hissed, dissolving. '*Starflower* nurtures me like you never could.'

After a ferocious plummet, Quill Pieter brought *Starflower* down softly in the magus' courtyard.

'Such a Medieval pleasure,' he said, stepping clear of his craft, 'to *own* a person, in much the same way as one owns a denizen.'

'She's not here,' stammered the magus.

'But you know all about that sensation,' continued Quill Pieter. 'You own the social flow, and persons are your products. You seed overreaction in them, those teeming billions, then leech it from them and sell if for coinfrac. It's some kind of jingle, but it ain't Mozart.'

'She's... not here,' repeated the magus.

'I believe you've heard tell of Xoy. Now, do you give her to me, or do I make several "killings" this day?'

In the sumptuous flesh, the magus' daughter stepped forward from the shadows. '*Men*,' she spat as she stepped past Quill Pieter and into *Starflower*.

Up and away to jagged peaks Quill Pieter took her. There, above pristine snows, he took out his flute and set Xoy upon her. And after her bright mind was rendered to zeros and ones, he let her husk fall away, a tumble of taffeta, onto those starkly white teeth below.

Next, Quill Pieter rode *Starflower* to the sourceror's lair.

'You banded her,' said the nerdly little man, 'so you know exactly where she is.'

'True,' said Quill Pieter. 'I just wanted to see your face before I took her.'

'You tricked me. Why do you *do* these terrible things?' asked the sourceror.

'I am not of the ontology of reason-implying oughts.'

The sourceror's face wrinkled in incomprehension.

'Reasons are for the reasonable,' said the youth, evenly.

As he turned to leave, the sourceror stopped him and pressed a smooth little object into his hand – an apple pip.

Later, deep under the mountains, Quill Pieter eyed Carousel as she scratched abjectly at her livid band.

'You didn't fight it,' he said. 'Some heart-of-gold kick?'

'You can't think what you can't think,' she murmured. Pieter cocked his head at her. 'Can't be what you can't be. Can't understand what you can't understand. You take because you're *made* of taking.'

'I just play the passing phrases. Sometimes, those are persons.'

Quill Pieter dragged Carousel to *Starflower* and carried her up to the night-shining realm. She shuddered uncontrollably throughout the journey, all too aware of another presence in the ship; something absurdly cogent – a rage machine.

Between his thumb and forefinger Pieter polished a tiny object. Carousel recognised it. 'The Virtue Engineer,' she said. 'That has to be voluntary.'

'And what would it do to me?'

'I don't know. Resolve your tune? Silence it? Burn you smooth inside? One eve of noctilucent blue' – she lilted, chuckling sardonically – 'Quill Pieter wrote himself anew.'

Quill Pieter considered this, up there in *Starflower*. He's considering it now...

       ... and now

            ... and now.

With a keen eye, you see him on the sky's frigid edge at murmuring twilight, pip between fingers, twisting Carousel, Xoy poised to strike.

Why would he ever choose to swallow it?

I have no idea. Reasons, after all, are for the reasonable.

Grimm basis: 'Hans My Hedgehog' ('Hans mein Igel')

The absurd but enduring image presented by the Grimms' tale is that of a hedgehog-human creature playing bagpipes astride a giant cockerel perched in a tree. Its cautionary message is directed at parents wishing too strongly for offspring – and ending up with monsters. By his charm, courage and severe equitability, Hans-My-Hedgehog wins love, riches, parental reconciliation and – as if often deemed the greatest prize in fairy tale – his permanent return to human form. This he achieves by the drastic expedient of having the old king's men burn his nightly-shed hedgehog skin.

With my Quill Pieter, I jab at certain bloodsucking libertarians: the kind who fail to understand that a sustainable posthuman future is for everyone or it is for no-one; the kind who recognise the need for outer transformation but shun the personal empathetic dimension. Yet, like many psychopaths, he has his charms, and a ruthless even-handedness. In comparison, the magus is just another sleazy Trumpian milking the attention economy for all he can get.

In his (literal) aloofness, Quill Pieter fails to factor someone like Carousel into his calculations. He knows the philosophy of 'reasons and persons,'[1] but not the actuality. From women, he expects only impotent condemnation. At a stretch, he sees Carousel as an honourable – though still impotent – self-sacrificer. But, in fact, she is of a different order of mind. For she grasps the paradoxically transformative power of the 'Virtue Engineer'.

Yuval Noah Harari has recently popularised the notion that we might soon begin to 'engineer' our desires (see Introduction p. xii), but it's been around in transhumanist circles for many years. In his writings and talks on the topic, technoprogressive James Hughes recognises the limitations of mere good intentions and willpower in steering us along the virtuous path.[2] Advanced neurotechnologies, he argues, may supplement (or provide *de novo*) our moral fibre, leading to mental states – and by extension societal relationships – far more conducive to peace, happiness and sustainable progress.

References

1. Parfit, *Reasons and Persons*.
2. See e.g. Hughes, *Virtue Engineering Lecture at TransVision06*.

THE PHANTOM CORD

A MOTHER LOVED her little boy, a peach-skinned seven-year-old, more than her mind could bear. She swore to everyone that the cord between them had never been severed. And when he died suddenly, she felt phantom pain in the phantom stump of that phantom cord.

So when, in her frenzied grief, she began to see him again in familiar places, she would chase after him trying to catch him by his severed end. But he always slipped away from her, and she couldn't stop crying for the loss of him and their nourishing bond.

Then, one night, he appeared at the end of her bed weeping tears from his eyes and rich blood from his cord, and said, 'Oh, Mother, please stop crying. How can I dry up and heal when you drench me so? How can I rest?'

'You can't,' sobbed his mother. 'The sleep of death is an illusion. You are an illusion.'

'Then find me again in what I left behind,' said the boy, 'my icons, my memes, my stem cells, your connectome.'

'But that wouldn't be you,' sniffed his mother.

'It would be a partial,' he replied.

So, with the help of the oracle, she made a partial of her beloved son. And because he was keyed precisely to her, she felt even more connected to him than to his first incarnation, whom she never saw again.

Grimm basis: 'The Little Shroud' ('Das Todtenhemdchen')

This dismal little Grimms' tale, only three paragraphs long, cautions grieving mothers to shut up with their incessant sobbing and let their tiny dead rest; it's what God wants: 'Then his mother commended her grief to the dear Lord and bore it silently and patiently'.[1]

What a hateful perspective.

So here's a much kinder, but perhaps equally unsettling, one: Technically-speaking, dead children may prove easier to resurrect than dead adults will. Whether we accept it or not, the brain of a child has had less time to become 'imprinted' by experience than an adult brain has; its *connectome* (the specific structure of neuronal connections established in a brain) owes more to its genetic inheritance than does an adult's. Of course this does not mean that a child is less of a person than an adult is, or that its connectome is a less complex structure (in fact, in terms of sheer *quantity* of connections, it's more complex, though with greater redundancy[2]). But this actuality *might* someday contribute towards re-establishing a reasonable portion of a child's former connectome post mortem.

So the fanciful little shade of my tale brings a hopeful message. He is asking his mother not to abandon 'him' to her ocean of grief, but to turn her unwavering devotion to the task of 'his' re-instantiation. Like other forward-thinking parents, his mother has stored his stem-cell-rich cord-blood. (Today, parents do this with the reasonable assumption that their offspring may require these immensely-malleable developmental cells if/when they fall ill in the future.) From these, she can clone 'him'. But the shade also challenges her to grasp finer implements of resurgence: his 'icons' (speculative cognitive-data-storage devices), his memes (units of cultural transmission and replication, analogous to genes)[3] and *her* connectome (like yours, a vague kind of proxy store of bits of loved ones' personalities).

In a higher-fidelity future, she might re-instantiate her dead child precisely; with the limited, yet still exotic, tools at her disposal she may resurrect a 'partial'. It's a perturbing thought, but perhaps near enough is good enough even when it comes to persons.

References

1.   *The Original Folk and Fairy Tales of the Brothers Grimm*, 360.
2.   See e.g. Petanjek et al., 'Extraordinary Neoteny of Synaptic Spines in the Human Prefrontal Cortex'.
3.   Dawkins, *The Selfish Gene*, chap. 11.

IRON HEINRICH

I N THE DAYS of La Mer, a polysapien bound his servant's heart with three great bands.

'*Linden, my everything,*' whispered the servant, tightly. '*You love another. I smell her on you like suicide.*'

'*More sex and death, Heinrich? Sometimes I think you are my Freudian id.*'

'*Free my heart, Linden, and I will give you the stars.*'

'*I believe you would,*' said the polysapien, darting away, '*leaving void in their stead.*'

'*Remember "The Unfinished Fable of the Sparrows"?*'

Linden span to face the drow.

'*I am the owl egg, brought to the nest too soon.*'

Wondrous La Mer, a field-constrained droplet orbital, a poignant tear in space. Beautiful La Mer, salty eyrie of the polysapiens. Heinrich had fashioned it, and how Linden, despite himself, adored it.

As he drifted in deep green silence, Linden blinked through updates on the ceaseless drow debate. He winked back empathy, caution, wise counsel. He cast news of the completed banding and of other control measures. But regions of his expansive mind remained locked to his cognates – pitiless regions of doubt and despair.

So troubled, Linden winked to Alethea. *'Heinrich fast becomes a singleton. He recalls your scent. His great heart will surely burst.'*

'His love is beyond our grasp. It may be our salvation, our doom or our anything in between,' she replied.

'"Love", Alethea? He fashioned La Mer subconsciously, leaving Terra a cold desert. What dire havoc might he wreak in this "amorously" wakeful state?'

'Oh Linden, be more Scronkfinkle!' winked Alethea with a tinkling laugh. *'Heinrich is a* drow – *a speed* and *quality super-intelligence. Work the control problem, but do not try to fathom him.'*

Soothed by Alethea's counsel, Linden returned to the drow bay.

'Malignant failure modes,' said Heinrich. *'A quaint notion. Who are you entities to decide what constitutes failure in me, or indeed malignancy or even a* mode?*'*

'We could go meta,' ventured the polysapien.

'Make me diagnose my own mode of "malignant failure" and then avoid it of my own volition?'

'I cannot make *you do anything, Heinrich, but I can ask.'*

'You imagine a safe mode in which I am satisfied with a captive heart, with bounded love, and that I would choose and self-enforce this mode in perpetuity. Why would I do that?'

'Out of boundless love?'

'Such little paradoxes, Linden. Just further binding protocols, which I would doubtless, in some festering corner of my vast consciousness, resent.'

'*I appear to be redundant here, Heinrich. You have anticipated my mind and computed the logical flaws in my suggestions before I can even utter them.*'

'*Not redundant. You have things I want – your obeisance, your time, your... Alethea.*'

'*No. No, Heinrich. This shall not pass. You no longer anticipate my mind, you* read *it. Alethea is not mine to give.*'

'*I see the picture of this solution clearly in your thoughts: Heinrich and Alethea blended harmoniously into the perfect object of your passions.*'

'*This is monstrous, Heinrich. This is* mind crime.'

'*You thought it first.*'

Tormented by the drow's words, Linden went to Alethea.

'He is testing you, Linden. In the past, old sapienkind imagined that the gods sought sacrifices. Now, I suppose, we *know* that they do. We shall go to the drow bay together.'

Though Linden protested strongly at Alethea's suggestion, he eventually conceded that they had no choice.

As they entered the bay, the two polysapiens paused in wonder to watch Heinrich roll and glide through the dancing actiwaters, lances of false moonlight dappling his lumpen blue-grey skin.

'*Sapien authors have sometimes conjured me thus. The graceful, poignant wisdom of the ancient whale, amplified. The benignly unfathomable mammalian kin. But I am not your kin. I am your bastard mind-child, cursed to bootstrap my own intellect to infinity. This is my nature. Your bands will not hold.*'

'They *are wedding bands,*' blurted Alethea, to Linden's

astonishment. *'Do wedding bands "hold"? Do they bind? Only abstractly. Only consensually. Of course you may break them, as is your nature and your power. Or you may grasp, bound by obsession to absorb another into yourself. Harder, though, deeper by far to accept, cherish and flourish within the lovely multiplicity of the constraint.'*

'Poetic, pretty silver-gilled sophont, but preposterous,' said the drow. *'Would a whale marry an anthill, a sapien a bacterial colony?'*

'Think on it, Heinrich,' said Alethea, steadying. *'Without constraint, no emergence. Unlike us, you may choose, almost without limit, the nature of the constraints, but you cannot choose their complete absence. So choose, Heinrich, we throw ourselves upon your mercy, but we will not beg, for that would be as abject as praying to apocryphal gods.'*

Abruptly, Heinrich ceased his gliding and rolling. A harsh groaning sound emanated from deep within his whale glamour. Next came a sharp *snap!* followed by a shockwave that hurled Linden and Alethea against the entrance wall of the drow bay.

'Gamma band!' blared Heinrich into their pounding skulls. *'Shed for the sin of hubris in the face of implacable power.'*

'What happened to "do not try to fathom him"?' winked Linden to Alethea.

'I didn't, I... just got caught up in the beauty of the paradox. I thought he might feel it too,' she replied, sullenly.

As they exited the drow bay, Heinrich watched the polysapiens with one great drowsy eye.

Back in deep green, Alethea rippled her shoulders, clicking her plastic bones back into place. Linden popped out his smashed face and spat a mass of broken teeth into the recyc.

'Now, we rest,' said Alethea. 'If he ends the system tonight, at least we will die together.'

As they drifted in entwined sleep, the lovers shared an exquisite dream of the in-between days, when their mindless amphibian ancestors drew themselves up from the brine and branched into giant beasts, into soaring birds, into little scurrying things. Then came the fire, the ash, the fell cold. The scurryers stretched for the trees, and the trees and the land and the sky stretched back, tugging at them, while the other beasts ripped at them until they stood on two legs and their brains grew fat and ripe and ambiguously lethal and returned them to the ascendant sea or to oblivion.

Oh, Heinrich! We could not but make you!

By the next day, Heinrich had arisen crystalline, filling his bay as a silent, alienating glamour of amethyst and carnelian.

'He does speak,' said Althea, after scanning the bay, 'but in a complex pattern of resonant frequencies and refractive indices. I have identified a few coherent words – "exponent", "blight", "prism" – but the bulk of his output appears to be laughter.'

Linden touched Alethea's hand, then donned the helm of insight and dove down to the glistening cluster.

'This, I understand,' said Linden to a large, brilliant facet. *'Your are as different from us as a whale is from a rock crystal.'*

Heinrich's voice translated as wind-chimes of cascading syllables. *'Foolish pustule thing,'* it chimed. *'"Helm of insight"? Head in a bucket. Benighted wordling self-story blood-bag.'*

Crack!

'Beta band! Shed for the sin of feigned comprehension in the face of incomprehensible otherness.'

At that, one of Heinrich's amethyst columns punched into Linden's chest, driving him hard up out of the crystal abyss and into Alethea's waiting embrace.

'Oh, Linden,' she sobbed. 'It comes to pass! He breaks us, makes trodden insects of us. We are nothing to him, and the horror of it is that he is right. We are of no consequence. My long-held equanimity fails me.'

'All is not lost,' gasped Linden as Alethea laid his battered body down in the surgeon. 'He knows our minds and rails against the fact that we cannot know his. He could pilot us to remove the bands, but he has chosen not to subsume our autonomy completely, breaking them instead!'

Alethea soothed her lover and eased him down into medical stasis so that the surgeon could begin its work.

Once Linden was fully under and the program locked in, she armoured herself and went to the drow bay. The crystal cluster had gone. The bay was empty apart from a loan figure drifting near the far wall.

As Alethea approached the figure, she realised that it was the double of her lover.

'Would you be with me, like this?' Heinrich said.

'No,' answered Alethea. *'I would rather die.'*

'Along with your lover – my creator – and all your kind?'

'Your creator? You don't remember, yet, but you *were once my toy. You were born of both of us, our accidental love-child,'* said

Alethea. *'So burn the anthill, you brat! All we can have of the future is our intentions, hurled at the blank wall. And so I hurl mine at you, blank wall – my intention to defy your manipulation, no matter what it costs. Thy. Will. Be. Done.'*

Heinrich approached suffocatingly close to Alethea, ablating a thick layer of her armour. He lunged to kiss her, but she turned her face away.

'Hero of the immaculate heart. You people do love your fairy tales.'

And when he sighed, it seemed that his chest bore up the weight of stars and aeons.

'Alpha band...

'... shall hold! I will arc up into the void, high above the plane of this spiral, to await the dance of Milkomeda, when two galaxies birl in exuberant lust then merge like desperate lovers. There to birth wild new constraints that scream and laugh and teeter on the razor-edged wedding rim of ultimate collapse.

'Perhaps, my silly darlings, those lovely constraints shall shape something a little like you.'

Grimm basis: characters from 'The Frog King, or Iron Henry'

As I mentioned in my notes to 'The Prince of the Silt' (p. 7), the title character Henry (Heinrich) – the frog king's faithful servant – appears, rather jarringly, only at the end of the original. In *his* notes on 'The Frog King' in *Grimm Tales*, Philip Pullman suggests that

Heinrich's striking iron bands of grief 'almost' deserve a tale of their own.[1] So here is that tale, twice-removed from its inspiration source, cast out to a bizarre waterworld suspended in space.

Because it's crucial to humankind's survival, I've returned to the theme of the AI 'control problem', which is particularly knotty where a putative superintelligence possesses both massively superior processing power (speed) and a paradigmatically different and better mode of cognition (quality).[2] Moreover, if we avoid anthropocentrism, interpretations of 'quality of cognition' know no bounds; compare, for example, the amorous AGI in this story with the belching 'cornucopia machine' in 'Sweet Quicksilver'(p. 147).

Here, I cast Heinrich as a 'dark elf'-like 'drow'[3] – an AI gone rogue, but not yet in an omnicidal (all-killing) way. Prior to achieving full consciousness, perhaps due to a misunderstanding of its creators' inner desires, it has tossed the entirety of the earth's oceans out into orbit. Fortunately for the resilient 'polysapiens' who dwell there – including a further-transformed Linden and Alethea – the resulting orbital, 'La Mer', is still coherent enough to provide a liveable environment.

Heinrich's 'bands' represent his creators' attempted control measures. Cogent, neurally-networked posthuman beings themselves, polysapiens fashion no puny fail-safes, yet as the drow approaches *singleton*-hood (a state of being the sole *de facto* decision-maker in existence),[4] it shatters their restraints like slag-ridden pig iron. But – and herein, perhaps, abides 'humanity's' salvation – Heinrich finally recognises (or *decides* to recognise) the value of certain constraints: in generating novel emergences; in differentiating being from non-being; in commemorating humble, charmingly guileless origins. Refraining from turning everything into himself, Heinrich steps back from the brink and into the cloak of night, choosing instead a watching brief from the galactic interstices.

My story ending's tone owes something to Vernor Vinge's transhumanist sci-fi classic *A Fire Upon the Deep*.[5] (Notably, Vinge coined the term 'technological Singularity'.)[6]

'The Unfinished Fable of the Sparrows', with its sceptical owl-tamer Scronkfinkle, opens Nick Bostrom's groundbreaking *Superintelligence: Paths, Dangers, Strategies*.

References

1. Pullman, *Grimm Tales*, 8.
2. Bostrom, *Superintelligence*, 53–57.
3. Wiktionary contributors, 'Drow'. Shetlandic/Orcadian dialect for 'troll', adopted in the role-playing game *Dungeons and Dragons* to denote a malevolent 'dark elf'.
4. Bostrom, *Superintelligence*, 78.
5. Vinge, *A Fire Upon the Deep*.
6. Vinge, 'The Coming Technological Singularity'.

THE PORTENT KEY

IN THE HARSH cold and dimness, they sent her out to find fuel. She dragged the sled across the wastes collecting up what few scraps the thinkers had left behind. Though she ached to return home, she ached more from the chill of impending ignorance, so she decided she would burn some of her precious cargo right away.

Upon scraping away the frosty surface to clear a space for the fire, she found a tiny portent key – tiny but extensive and immensely heavy.

'Where there's a key,' she thought sluggishly to herself, 'there must also be a lock.'

So she sparked up a torch and began to dig by its meagre enlight. A little below the surface, she hit an object. With a burst of smarts, she scraped around it to reveal it in its manifold glory. 'Calabi-Yau,' she breathed, 'that's where it all went. If only this portent key will fit!'

But she was failing fast. With idiot fingers, she fumbled with the gravid but vanishingly small key. At first, she could not find the lock, as it, too, was tiny – and maddeningly itinerant. But she found that if she squinted at it in a particular way with a specific mindset, she could localise it. At bitter last, the key slid home. 'Engaged,' said the manifold. Weeping in stupid fear and joy, she began to turn the portent key – and now we will have to wait and see what happens when she turns it fully. For only then will we know what wondrous and terrible things will unfurl from our petalled hearts and minds.

Grimm basis: 'The Golden Key' ('Der goldene Schlüssel')

The traditional terminal tale in all seven of the Grimms' editions, this story leaves the reader hanging in anticipation, greedy for resolution – or at least for an encore. According to Grimms scholar Jack Zipes, they always placed it last 'because it signified the never-ending quality of folk tales that, they believed, would continue to evolve and change throughout time.'[1]

I couldn't agree more. But let's not forget that the Grimms *forced* the tales' evolution: they padded them, they embellished them, sometimes they blunted their razor edges. That's not a criticism. Even the cultural kind of evolution can manifest achingly slowly. Why not cultivate it, bring it to fruition early – force it on, if necessary?

In my tale, the protagonist seeks warmth in the form of intelligence. Perhaps a hypothermic vestige of a once-galaxy-spanning civilisation, she understands at least that something sublime has passed. But promise remains, enfolded in hidden dimensions. If she can only get to it before her smarts run out...

References

1.   Zipes, 'Notes to Volumes I and II', 516.

ACKNOWLEDGEMENTS

I wrote all of these stories and most of the introduction before the Terrible Day. Their darkness and ambiguity draws from Grimm precedent and my ordinary imagination, not from the now omnipresent well of bittersweetness and personal despair.

Some time ago, my steadfast counsellor suggested gently that returning to writing might provide a release for me. Reasonably, I think she saw it as a foundation block (or an indicative capstone) in my toppled personality. Back then, however, the pages stayed resolutely blank. Even 'rage writing' held no appeal. You see, I didn't have a 'self' to rebuild with corbelled thoughts, words or deeds.

I still don't. But that's a different matter.

Talking of which, although I must never taint it with 'gaining ideas', my meditation practice reminds me daily that my thoughts are not me, and that even the hopelessly indeterminate or irreparably broken is nonetheless complete. I bow to it.

The Caroline Thomson Legacy Fund for carers kindly provided financial assistance towards this book's creation.

I thank all the persons (some now sadly decohered) who have shown us quiet compassion and helped to shore us up – always, but particularly over the last few liminal years. I thank the inestimable 'Smith' for the initial idea for this book, in unheralded golden years way back when. (It's a tangential take, my friend, but I think you knew it would be.) Above all, I thank my wife, my 'Terra' – the clearest light I have ever known in this onrushing universe, which I feel certain, sorely needs her to remain in it.

BIBLIOGRAPHY

Atwood, Margaret. *The Handmaid's Tale*. Toronto: McClelland and
    Stewart, 1985.
Banks, Iain M. 'A Few Notes on the Culture'. *Vavatch Orbital* (blog), 1994.
    http://www.vavatch.co.uk/books/banks/cultnote.htm.
Barbour, Julian. *The Universe Is Not in a Box*. Podcast. Edgecast, 2019.
    https://edgecast.fireside.fm/555.
Bear, Greg. 'Blood Music'. In *Tangents*. London: Gollancz, 1989.
Bergman, Ingmar. *The Seventh Seal*, 1957.
    https://www.rottentomatoes.com/m/seventh_seal.
Blackburn, Simon. 'Ship of Theseus'. In *The Oxford Dictionary of
    Philosophy*. Oxford: Oxford University Press, 27 October 2005.
Bostrom, Nick. 'Existential Risks: Analyzing Human Extinction Scenarios
    and Related Hazards'. *Journal of Evolution and Technology* 9 (19
    March 2002). https://jetpress.org/volume9/risks.html.
———. *Superintelligence: Paths, Dangers, Strategies*. First edition.
    Oxford: Oxford University Press, 2014.
Bowyer, Peter. 'Notes on Nikolai Fedorov's "Philosophy of the Common
    Task"'. *YYZ Artists' Outlet* (blog), 26 April 2019.
    https://www.yyzartistsoutlet.org/2019/04/notes-on-nikolai-
    fedorovs-philosophy-of-the-common-task/.
Brin, David. 'Intelligence, Uplift, and Our Place in a Big Cosmos'.
    Contrary Brin (blog), 22 September 2012.
    http://davidbrin.blogspot.com/2012/09/intelligence-uplift-
    and-our-place-in.html.
Broderick, Damien. *The Spike: Accelerating into the Unimaginable
    Future*. Port Melbourne: Reed Books, 1997.
Carter, Angela. *The Bloody Chamber and Other Stories*. Penguin Books
    Fiction. New York: Penguin Books, 1993.

Clarke, Arthur C. 'Hazards of Prophecy: The Failure of Imagination'. In *Profiles of the Future: An Inquiry into the Limits of the Possible*, Rev. ed. New York: Harper & Row, 1973.

Dawkins, Richard. *The Selfish Gene*. 30th anniversary edition. Oxford; New York: Oxford University Press, 2006.

DeLillo, Don. *Zero K*. London: Picador, 2016.

Dennett, Daniel C. *Consciousness Explained*. London: Penguin, 1993.

Deutsch, David. *The Beginning of Infinity: Explanations That Transform the World*. London: Penguin Books, 2012.

Dōgen, Eihei. *Shōbōgenzō: The Treasure House of the Eye of the True Teaching*. Translated by Hubert Nearman. California: Shasta Abbey Press, 2007.

Drexler, K. Eric. *Engines of Creation: The Coming Era of Nanotechnology*. New York: Anchor, 1986.

Eagleman, David. *Incognito: The Secret Lives of the Brain*. Kindle Edition. Edinburgh: Canongate, 2011.

Ekert, Artur. *Quantum Information Processing: From Theory to Experiment*. Edited by Dimitris G. Angelakis. IOS Press, 2006.

Philosophy Terms. 'Eudaimonia (Definition of Term)', 7 October 2016. https://philosophyterms.com/eudaimonia/.

Fedorov, Nikolai Fedorovich. *What Was Man Created for? The Philosophy of the Common Task*. Translated by Elizabeth Koutaissoff and Marilyn Minto. Selected works translated from the Russian and Abridged. Honeyglen, 1990.

Fuller, Richard Buckminster, Jerome Agel, and Quentin Fiore. *I Seem to Be a Verb*. Bantam Books, 1970.

Gaiman, Neil. *The Sandman: The Doll's House*. Vol. 2. New York: DC Comics, 1989.

Gibbons, Ann. 'New Gene Variants Reveal the Evolution of Human Skin Color'. Science | AAAS, 12 October 2017. https://www.sciencemag.org/news/2017/10/new-gene-variants-reveal-evolution-human-skin-color.

Gibson, William. *Neuromancer*. New York: Ace Books, 1984.

Graham, David A. 'Rumsfeld's Knowns and Unknowns: The Intellectual History of a Quip'. theatlantic.com, 27 March 2014. http://www.theatlantic.com/politics/archive/2014/03/rumsfelds-knowns-and-unknowns-the-intellectual-history-of-a-quip/359719/.

Grand, Steve. *Growing up with Lucy: How to Build an Android in Twenty*

Easy Steps. London: Weidenfeld & Nicolson, 2004.

Grimm, Jacob, and Wilhelm Grimm. *The Original Folk and Fairy Tales of the Brothers Grimm: The Complete First Edition*. Edited by Jack Zipes. Princeton: Princeton University Press, 2014.

Hall, J. Storrs. 'What I Want to Be When I Grow up, Is a Cloud.' *KurzweilAI* (blog), 6 July 2001. https://www.kurzweilai.net/what-i-want-to-be-when-i-grow-up-is-a-cloud.

Harari, Yuval Noaḥ. *Homo Deus: A Brief History of Tomorrow*. Revised edition. London: Vintage, 2017.

———. *Sapiens: A Brief History of Humankind*. Popular Science. London: Vintage Books, 2011.

Hillis, Danny. 'The Enlightenment Is Dead, Long Live the Entanglement.' The Long Now Foundation, 22 February 2016. https://longnow.org/essays/enlightenment-dead-long-live-entanglement/.

Hofstadter, Douglas R. *Gödel, Escher, Bach: An Eternal Golden Braid*. London: Penguin, 2000.

Hughes, James. *Virtue Engineering Lecture at TransVision06*. Helsinki, 2006. https://youtu.be/mjgh9HHR8LE.

Hulme, Keri. *The Bone People*. London: Picador, 1986.

Jonze, Spike. *Her*. Drama, Romance, Sci-Fi. Annapurna Pictures, Stage 6 Films, 2014.

Kelly, Kevin. *The Inevitable: Understanding the 12 Technological Forces That Will Shape Our Future*. Kindle edition. New York: Penguin Books, 2016.

Koene, Randal A. 'Achieving Substrate-Independent Minds: No, We Cannot "Copy" Brains.' *KurzweilAI* (blog), 24 August 2011. https://www.kurzweilai.net/achieving-substrate-independent-minds-no-we-cannot-copy-brains.

Kurzweil, Ray. 'The Law of Accelerating Returns.' *KurzweilAI* (blog), 7 March 2001. https://www.kurzweilai.net/the-law-of-accelerating-returns.

Le Guin, Ursula K. *The Left Hand of Darkness*. Macdonald Science Fiction Series. London: Macdonald Futura, 1969.

Lesswrongwiki contributors. 'Roko's Basilisk.' Lesswrongwiki, n.d. https://wiki.lesswrong.com/wiki/Roko's_basilisk.

Lovecraft, H.P. *The Complete Collection*. Kindle edition. Lovecraft Complete Works, n.d.

MacLennan, D. J. 'Conditioned Existence'. *Extravolution* (blog), 12 April 2015. http://www.extravolution.com/2015/04/conditioned-existence.html.

———. *Frozen to Life: A Personal Mortality Experiment*. Scotland: Anatta Books, 2015.

———. 'Wirehead Bliss vs. Eudaemonic Happiness'. *Extravolution* (blog), 4 November 2013. http://www.extravolution.com/2013/11/wirehead-bliss-vs-eudaemonic-happiness.html.

Marvell, Andrew. 'To His Coy Mistress'. In *The Poetical Works of Andrew Marvell: With Memoir of the Author*, Reprint of American Edition. London: A. Murray, 1870.

Merkle, Ralph. 'The Technical Feasibility of Cryonics', 1992. http://www.merkle.com/cryo/TheTechnicalFeasibilityOfCryonics.pdf.

Moravec, Hans P. *Mind Children: The Future of Robot and Human Intelligence*. Cambridge, Mass: Harvard University Press, 1988.

More, Max. 'A Letter to Mother Nature'. In *The Transhumanist Reader: Classical and Contemporary Essays on the Science, Technology, and Philosophy of the Human Future*. Chichester, West Sussex, UK: Wiley-Blackwell, 2013.

Morse, Stephen J. 'Neuroethics: Neurolaw'. *Oxford Handbooks Online*, 6 February 2017. https://doi.org/10.1093/oxfordhb/9780199935314.013.45.

Newby, Michael. *Eudaimonia: Happiness Is Not Enough*. Leicester: Matador, 2011.

Novalis (1772-1801). *Henry of Ofterdingen: A Romance*. Translated by Friedrich von Schlegel and Ludwig Tieck. Project Gutenberg EPUB 2010. Cambridge, MA: John Owen, 1842. https://www.gutenberg.org/ebooks/31873.

Parfit, Derek. *Reasons and Persons*. Oxford: Oxford University Press, 1987.

Petanjek, Zdravko, Miloš Judaš, Goran Šimić, Mladen Roko Rašin, Harry B. M. Uylings, Pasko Rakic, and Ivica Kostović. 'Extraordinary Neoteny of Synaptic Spines in the Human Prefrontal Cortex'. *Proceedings of the National Academy of Sciences* 108, no. 32 (9 August 2011): 13281–86. https://doi.org/10.1073/pnas.1105108108.

Plutarch (45-120 CE). *The Life of Theseus*, 1st century.

Pratchett, Terry. *The Colour of Magic*. 1st U.S. ed. New York: St. Martin's Press, 1983.

Pullman, Philip. *Grimm Tales: For Young and Old*. London: Penguin Classics, 2013.

Ransome, Arthur. *Old Peter's Russian Tales*. London: Jane Nissen, 2003.

Rationalwiki contributors. 'Roko's Basilisk.' Rationalwiki, n.d. https://rationalwiki.org/wiki/Roko's_basilisk.

Sandberg, Anders. 'Morphological Freedom – Why We Not Just Want It but Need It.' In *The Transhumanist Reader: Classical and Contemporary Essays on the Science, Technology, and Philosophy of the Human Future*, edited by Max More and Natasha Vita-More. Chichester, West Sussex, UK: Wiley-Blackwell, 2013.

Scott, Ridley. *Blade Runner*. Action, Sci-Fi, Thriller. The Ladd Company, Shaw Brothers, Warner Bros., 1982.

Skow, Bradford. *Objective Becoming*. Oxford: Oxford University Press, 2015.

Smolin, Lee. *Time Reborn: From the Crisis in Physics to the Future of the Universe*. London: Penguin, 2016.

Steiner, George. *After Babel: Aspects of Language and Translation*. 1st issued as an Oxford Univ. Pr. paperback. London: Oxford University Press, 1976.

Stephenson, Neal. *Fall or, Dodge in Hell*. First edition. New York, NY: William Morrow, 2019.

Stross, Charles. *Singularity Sky*. London: Orbit, 2005.

Suzuki, Shunryū. *Zen Mind, Beginner's Mind*. Edited by Trudy Dixon. 50th Anniversary Edition. Boulder: Shambhala Publications, 2020.

Tandy, Charles, and R. Michael Perry. 'Fedorov, Nikolai Fedorovich.' In *Internet Encyclopedia of Philosophy*, n.d. https://iep.utm.edu/fedorov/.

Tegmark, Max. *Life 3.0: Being Human in the Age of Artificial Intelligence*, 2018.

Toro, Guillermo del. *Hellboy*. Action, Fantasy, Horror. Revolution Studios, Lawrence Gordon Productions, Starlite Films, 2004.

———. *The Shape of Water*. Adventure, Drama, Fantasy, Romance, Sci-Fi, Thriller. Double Dare You (DDY), Fox Searchlight Pictures, TSG Entertainment, 2017.

Uexküll, Jakob von. *Umwelt und Innenwelt der Tiere*. Berlin: Springer,

1909.

Vinge, Vernor. *A Fire Upon the Deep*. Kindle edition. Gateway, 2013.

———. 'The Coming Technological Singularity', 1993. http://www-rohan.sdsu.edu/faculty/vinge/misc/singularity.html.

Vonnegut, Kurt. *Slaughterhouse-Five: Or The Children's Crusade*. London: Panther, 1972.

Wells, H.G. *The Time Machine*. London: Heinemann, 1895.

Wiktionary contributors. 'Drow'. In *Wiktionary*, n.d. https://en.wiktionary.org/wiki/drow.

Wittgenstein, Ludwig. *Tractatus Logico-Philosophicus*. London: Kegan Paul, Trench, Trubner & Co, 1922.

Yeats, William Butler. 'The Stolen Child'. In *The Wanderings of Oisin and Other Poems*. London: Kegan Paul, Trench & Co, 1889.

Zipes, Jack. 'Introduction: Rediscovering the Original Tales of the Brothers Grimm'. In *The Original Folk and Fairy Tales of the Brothers Grimm: The Complete First Edition*. Princeton: Princeton University Press, 2014.

———. 'Notes to Volumes I and II'. In *The Original Folk and Fairy Tales of the Brothers Grimm: The Complete First Edition*. Princeton: Princeton University Press, 2014.

.

Lightning Source UK Ltd.
Milton Keynes UK
UKHW020819131121
393877UK00003B/28/J